SENSUAL
SECRETS

SENSUAL
SECRETS

Anonymous

Translated from the French by
Alan Shipway

W H ALLEN · LONDON
1989

Translation copyright © Nexus Books 1989

Printed and bound in Great Britain by
Mackays of Chatham PLC, Chatham, Kent
for the Publishers, W.H. Allen & Co. Plc
Sekforde House, 175/9 St John Street, London EC1V 4LL

ISBN 0 491 03834 8

Contents

Sensual Secrets

Foreword

Love, as everyone knows, is a mixture of feelings which are more or less deep and physical sensations which are more or less intense, according to the nature of the people experiencing them.

Everybody knows something about such feelings, has experienced them at least once in their life: emotions bordering upon a state of illness, irrational exaltation causing one to cherish, to esteem, to admire even the slightest gestures of the beloved object and the desire to be the only one in his or her heart.

All these feelings, which are sometimes ardent, sometimes tender, are experienced in the same way by both sexes, with this difference that the man expresses his emotions more violently than the woman.

But the similarity which exists in the problems of the heart is far from subsisting in the second of love's domains – that of the senses.

Physiologically, the 'male' being is as different from the 'female' being as the day is from the night. But everyone knows that.

A great deal has been said about this subject, an equal number of basic truths and stupid opinions has been accumulated: 'Man is made to give, woman to receive,' (malicious!) or, 'In love the man dominates, the woman submits.'

9

All these observations, inspired by La Palisse, can quite easily be inverted. How many women maintain that, contrary to all Nature's laws, it is they who give, since they 'give themselves,' and, consequently, dominate the game! Truly there are no absolute rules when one goes beyond the merely physical. But, limiting ourselves strictly to the sphere of bodily attraction, we can confidently affirm that physical love between two people does not have at all the same features when considered from the point of view of one or the other partner.

Embracing . . . two bodies which entwine, grip each other, caress each other, sometimes lasciviously, sometimes violently; two naked bodies quivering harmoniously in their efforts to attain the supreme satisfaction, sobbing like panic-stricken beasts.

That is the point of view of the poet, who puts the embrace into just one picture, who unites man and woman under the single emblem of Love without distinguishing different kinds of voluptuousness.

That is all well and good . . . The act of love has been glorified precisely because of this union which, as the poet says, 'transforms two bodies into one being'.

But has anyone ever attempted to analyse this embrace, considering in detail the pleasure of the male and of the female?

It seems to me that this is a real challenge. Until now the most beautiful pages of love have only given a general picture of the act, describing the voluptuous feelings of either the man or the woman.

The author of this book has left the beaten track and is presenting not only an audacious work to his readers but also a novelty.

This love story (a true one) is not just limited to the various stages of carnal possession and its magnificent sensations. For the embraces which come to life are narrated first of all by the young lady, who describes exquisite feelings with all the frankness of a heart conquered by love; next, the young man relives the same scene, giving us his triumphantly male impressions.

Truly, this is an unusual book and likely to win the favour of those readers who are eager for the new and the unexpected. For this procedure, which has never before been used, will be a veritable revelation to them!

From chapter to chapter, from the miraculous birth of love until the apotheosis of its carnal voluptuousness, the same scenes will be lived first by the woman, then by the man with the same total frankness.

Readers, what does it matter to you whether the author of this book is a man or a woman? All that you need to know is that the most scrupulous preparation and the most rigorous documentation preceded the composition of the work.

A subtle, intelligent and sensual man; a sensitive, passionate, magnificently beautiful woman were the confidants of the writer. And it is what they confided to him that his pen will bring to life: intimate secrets whispered by the soft, warm lips of a passionate woman, graver secrets born of a man's love for that same woman.

The timorous or the hypocritical should abstain from reading such things: for frankness, which is the lover's prime quality, permeates this story and confers upon it an absolute realism.

I

Saturday, 12th June, 1937.

SHE

How lovely! Free at last! A month, a whole long month to rest, to calm my overwrought nerves, to be reborn! How happy I am!

Oh, to be sure, I have no right to complain! Other women would undoubtedly envy me. To be twenty-five, to be (it seems) pretty, and also free, divorced, to possess a little money, to exercise the profession of mannequin for a famous Parisian dress-designer solely to avoid the boredom consequent upon too much leisure and also with a view to possible adventures, isn't all that enough to make a woman happy?

And yet, in spite of all the attractions of such an existence, it only half pleases me. I have had enough of that hollow, brilliant life, of that perpetual agitation in the world of the capital and of its pleasures. Enough of futile chit-chat with the lovely girls who are my colleagues; enough of cocktails in the bars of the Madeleine with little old men whose only interest is to get into bed with me; enough of exhibiting dresses at the weigh-in at Longchamp and during week-ends at Deauville; enough of snobbery, of insipid compliments, of the odours of dance-halls. In that deceptive life, I have found only momentary stimulation, artificial pleasures which never satisfy me fully.

It's like love . . . that grand word which is uttered with such respect: what is it for me, that love triumphant? Nothing very joyful, until now. In short, I'm a disappointed woman.

My marriage with a man considerably older than myself brought me nothing but disgust. My husband? A cynical, impotent man, who gazed upon my naked body with bloodshot eyes, who demanded shameful caresses, which did not however succeed in rekindling long dead flames.

The day I discovered him with the maid sitting on his lap while he thrust an eager and trembling hand up her skirt came as a great relief to me: a golden opportunity to divorce him, the liberation which I had been secretly longing for!

But for a long time my new-found freedom seemed to lack savour, so much had I been disgusted by that unpleasant experience! It was only when several months had gone by that I began to react, that I started to try to do something, to occupy myself, to forget that ordeal by intoxicating myself with pleasures.

Ah, the lovers I had! Frank to the point of boldness, longing to find love, I didn't hesitate to throw myself into the arms of anyone who seemed to want me. But no one brought me the hoped-for revelation. Every adventure left me a little more bruised, a little more disillusioned than before!

The men I've known! Brazen gigolos with minds enfeebled by an excessive amount of sport, robust males who thought they were perfect lovers but whose fatuity had blinded them or addled their brains, old men with shameful passions and well-filled wallets!

13

They were all much of a muchness: zero, zero for all those puppets, who were unable to distinguish a sensual woman from a tart!

Two years passed, two years of abortive seeking, disappointed hopes and sterile embraces . . . And now my ideas and my feelings have changed: I'm tired of seeking, tired of ceaselessly chasing after men with an openness which has often led to me being taken for a professional practitioner of the art of love. For some time now my womanly modesty has returned. The last three months have been notable for virtue and abstinence: I have reconstituted my virginity!

It was in this state of mind that I arrived yesterday in this little village in the Pyrenees for a month's holiday. What happiness to feel born anew, no longer to worry about anything but eating and sleeping and admiring the lovely scenery! Enough of Parisian life, bars and fashionable parties! I feel myself to be another woman.

This morning I opened the window and sunlight came flooding into the room, caressing me like a lover! Resting my elbows on the window-sill, surrounded by flowers and climbing-plants, I contemplated the countryside which was still shrouded in the mist of early morning. The White Horse Hotel, where I am staying, faces the small village square: a shady and charming place, with an ancient rustic fountain and benches upon which old countrymen sit and doze peacefully. A bit farther on, rising above the roofs with their russet tiles, one can see the spire of the village church, straight as a prayer in the clear June sky. On the horizon one can see the rather vague outline of mountains whose distant summits are crowned with eternal snow, which is as pure as my heart this radiant morning!

14

After having spent some considerable time admiring that dream-like landscape, I wandered around my room humming, a cigarette between my lips. Passing in front of the wardrobe mirror, I caught sight of my smiling reflection and felt a sudden urge to contemplate that reflection in intimate detail.

The négligée caressed my smooth shoulders as it slipped down and fell at my feet in a lacy corolla. There I was naked, completely naked in front of the mirror: and the picture that presented itself to me in the pitch-pine frame filled me with intense happiness.

I know that I am beautiful . . . Men have often told me so. I was even awarded the title of *The most beautiful mannequin in Paris*! And yet, I'm a bit like Saint Thomas: I need to see to be convinced. Was it really me, that lovely, tall, smiling girl, as elegantly curved as a Tanagra? Was it really mine, that long, supple body with its marvellously smooth white skin, that firm pale body, so proud in its nudity? Without false shame I admired my breasts, which are harmoniously rounded, and whose points at that moment were erect; an inexplicable coquetry causes me to put rouge on them! And my stomach, so flat, smooth as polished marble, leading down to that place between my thighs which is covered by a fleece as golden as a field of corn in the sunshine. And then my thighs, a little on the plump side, with the tiny beauty spot which I laughingly call 'my trade mark,' a minuscule brown stain nestling high up on the thigh, close to the silken hair of my sex.

I turned round and could now admire the full curves of my hips, unblemished white globes of warm flesh separated by a dark, mysterious furrow and crowned by seductive dimples! At one time I used to blush because of my over-developed bottom; but now I'm

15

proud of it because men's eyes are irresistibly drawn to my behind as I walk.

My face came next; I scrutinized its reflected image in the mirror. A thin, pale face, skilfully made up however, with a dainty nose whose nostrils were sensitive, a sensual mouth, very red, like a bloodstain, and eyes . . . eyes of which I am justly proud: they are immense and green like the dangerous depths of the sea under my carefully plucked eyebrows. Those eyes confer a wildness, a strangeness upon me that forms a happy contrast with my golden hair which is artfully arranged and delightfully curly.

You should be satisfied with this examination, Jacqueline, you're not at all bad-looking! And in spite of my present chastity, I couldn't help thinking that such a perfect body, such perverse features were made for voluptuous embraces. Heaven grant that I shall at last meet the man who can fully satisfy me, who will make me his slave of love, marked by the burning brand of pleasure!

The fine weather prompted me to go for a walk before lunch. I considered what to wear, for even in this rustic corner, I wanted to be coquettish, to make myself beautiful in order to celebrate the joy which dwelt in my heart.

First of all, the underwear. I fastened a delicate suspender-belt of pale blue satin around my waist.

Next came the knickers. My capricious hands foraged amongst a pile of lingerie, finally choosing a dear little pair of blue silk embroidered with pale yellow lace. I'm in the habit of wearing very clinging knickers, two sizes smaller than I should wear, for I love to feel them hugging me: it is my besetting sin to savour the delightful caress of silk on my bottom, the indiscreet penetration of the tissue into the most secret parts of my body.

I was now wearing the knickers. I admired the elegant woman in the mirror, who looked perversely attractive in her underclothes. My belly and buttocks were tightly moulded by the clinging knickers. One could clearly distinguish the outline of my sex through the fine silk and the furrow between the cheeks of my derrière.

Should I wear the pretty lace brassière? No, there is no reason to do so: my arrogantly firm breasts need no support. So I put on a charming blouse of white silk whose contact immediately caused the rouged points of my breasts to harden.

A very tight brown skirt, a little matching jacket harmoniously completed my dressing. Just a touch more lipstick, a bit more mascara on my eye-lashes and I went out into the square.

How good it was! The mountain breeze invigorated me and kissed my face like a barbaric lover. I offered myself to the wind and the sunshine, gave them my body unreservedly and the breeze moulded my clothes to my body as though intent upon revealing all!

With long strides I walked about the streets of the village laughing with care-free abandon at everything I saw. I felt free of all constraint like a woman who has just been satisfied by her lover . . . and those naughty little knickers stimulated me deliciously between my thighs as I walked and caressed my bottom like a hand wearing a silken glove.

A tourist appeared: he passed me, walking with long strides as I did. His elegant appearance left me in no doubt that he too was a visitor here. He was wearing plus-fours and a suède jacket but he did not have a hat. I looked at him quite boldly and found

17

him very pleasing! Thirty or perhaps thirty-two, clean-shaven with well-marked features, black hair combed back from his forehead, and beautiful brown eyes that a sensitive woman would like to see light up with pleasure as they gazed upon her naked body . . . My word, what a good-looking young man!

As we passed each other, our eyes met for a few seconds; and in those of the stranger I saw an expression which was at once so intense and so strange, that I felt myself blushing. Was I becoming shy?

The rest of my walk was haunted by that meeting which had awakened a kind of sweet portent, as yet rather vague in my heart.

I went back to The White Horse Hotel and made my way to the rustic dining-room where lunch was being served. What a pleasant surprise! The handsome stranger who I had encountered in the village sat all by himself at a table near the window. I might have guessed that he would be staying here!

I installed myself at another table which was very close to his and sat there almost facing him. It seemed to me that a sort of complicity had already established itself between us.

It is no my intention to weary you with a detailed description of that meal which I hardly tasted so conscious was I of the young man's eyes upon me, scrutinizing me, undressing me. I felt as if he was already possessing me and quivered in anticipation.

By the time the dessert arrived the ice was broken. Using some futile pretext, the stranger spoke to me. And almost immediately added

'Have you been here long, mademoiselle?'

'Since yesterday evening.'

'Well, what a coincidence! Me too! And I'll bet you're from Paris. With such elegance!'

'Quite right. And you, monsieur, are you a Parisian too?'

'Yes, I am. I'm having a month's rest here.'

A month . . . the same as me! A thrill of pleasure ran through my whole being and, in spite of myself, I blushed.

Now we were chattering away together like old friends . . . or future lovers. The young man's name is Michel Semblier, and he is an artist residing at Paris. He must be wealthy judging from his manners, his easy confidence and also, as I was to see shortly, his car, a luxurious Renault slumbering in front of the hotel.

After we had had our coffee and liqueurs, we were both seized by a momentary embarrassment. Obviously, we were both acutely aware of the question which was about to be asked:

'Have you any plans for this afternoon?'

'Not yet, monsieur. Have you?'

He hesitated for a moment.

'Perhaps we could go for a walk together? There's going to be a fair in the village. It must be very picturesque. Would you do me the honour of accompanying me?'

'It would give me the greatest pleasure. But if you wouldn't mind waiting for a few moments, I'd like to change my dress. . . . It's so hot!'

I hastened to my room all aglow with an indefinable pleasure. I quickly slipped out of my skirt, jacket and blouse and put on a very light flowered summer dress with a wide skirt. I should feel more comfortable in that. I repaired my make-up, satisfied an urgent need in the bathroom, then rejoined my cavalier.

19

In the village square the fair was in full swing. It was a charming travelling fair with its lotteries, its shooting-galleries, its wooden horses and swings. Crowds of people were there, dressed in their Sunday-best. The air was filled with deafening mechanical music, which I found quite exciting.

Our first stop was at a shooting-gallery. My companion proposed that we should have a competition. But I am not a good shot and did very badly. Michel, on the contrary, is a Nimrod of the highest order. He scored a bullseye every time he fired, with an unerring sureness which was quite remarkable.

We went to the swings after that: they're what I like best at fairs. Unfortunately, my escort hated them because, he told me, they made him feel nauseous. However, he didn't want to spoil my pleasure and insisted upon my having a go without him while he waited for me. Soon I was swinging merrily back and forth. How good it felt! The many colours and sights of the fair became jumbled together as I moved faster and faster. Acting upon a sudden impulse, intoxicated by the speed and the wind, I stood up. But straight away that wind caused my skirt to balloon out around me. Undoubtedly my undergarments could be seen from below. What a pleasure for me! Certainly my bare thighs must be visible and, perhaps, some of the lace of my knickers! Down below all the men were gazing up at what was being revealed to them, their faces flushed with desire. And I wondered what impression I was making on Michel.

What ought I to do? Sit down? Cover my thighs with my skirt? But they might think that I had something shameful to hide! And anyway, I didn't give a damn about modesty! An intense voluptuousness took possession of me at the idea that Michel could see my

20

intimate undergarments. But would he think that I was just a tart? Perhaps, but it didn't seem important. Intoxicated with joy, I continued to swing back and forth, cheeks flushed, hair blown by the wind, skirt up around my waist. The feel of the cool air caressing my bare thighs sent a thrill of desire through me.

Eventually, I descended from the swing, somewhat ashamed of my brazen behaviour. Michel gazed at me with an expression of intense desire. His face was very flushed, even though he had not been on the swing.

'How about having a go on the roundabout?' he said.

I agreed enthusiastically. It was a very fine merry-go-round, equipped with splendid horses which were already being mounted by a swarm of village girls and arrogant young soldiers.

One horse was free: we both climbed onto it: that is to say, Michel leapt on effortlessly and indicated that I should install myself in front of him. Laughingly I straddled the docile mount, the result of which was that my skirt was hitched up to the middle of my thighs. My big, lightly-clad bottom pressed down on the varnished wood which struck cold through the thin skirt and knickers. Michel pressed himself against me from behind and I could feel his belly against my buttocks, which was not at all a disagreeable sensation!

To the accompaniment of the sounds of mechanical music, the roundabout got under way. On the pretext of preventing me from falling, my companion put his arms around me and his hands lightly cupped my gently rounded breasts. In fact, Michel was behaving like a soldier with a servant-girl! But I didn't take offence; the atmosphere of the fair made everything excusable.

For a long time we went round and round pressed

closely to each other. Laughing with a childlike joy, I leaned back a little until I could feel Michel's warm breath on the nape of my neck. Was it the wooden horse which was making me feel so strange? I think there was another reason . . .

I can't say for certain how long we stayed at the fair, nor am I sure how long we spent afterwards wandering along sinuous footpaths in the green meadows. We chattered away indefatigably and, to be honest, I no longer knew what I should do: should I just let things take their course and perhaps run the risk of being taken for a woman of easy virtue by my companion? Or should I behave with more constraint and let him think that my intention was to remain virtuous? It must be said that the second attitude would be entirely false. So in the end I decided to act naturally, to be myself, without worrying about conventions: for an obscure instinct made me realize that I should be his . . .

When we returned to the hotel, the setting sun was already turning the mountain crests a fiery hue. The old wooden stairs creaked under our feet. In the dark and silent corridor Michel put his hands on my shoulders.

'I can't tell you how delighted I am to have met you in this forgotten corner,' he murmured. 'Unfortunately, I shan't be dining here this evening: some friends who live locally have invited me to their chalet.'

The disappointment that this news caused me must have been plain to see, because I could see a smile on Michel's lips, in spite of the darkness. Gently he pulled me closer. My body was now pressing against his, and I felt helpless in those strong arms. He was going to kiss me, I could sense it. What would he think of me if I didn't resist? He would take me for a tart, without a doubt!

There was no longer any time to think about this problem, for Michel was bending over me, his eyes aflame with desire. How I loved that face, those greedy lips bent on capturing mine! All thought of resistance was banished. Michel pressed his mouth to mine, gently at first but with increasing authority. A voluptuous thrill ran through me, my nipples stiffened and in its silken covering my most intimate femininity melted with pleasure. My lips parted slightly. . . . Michel boldly thrust his tongue into my mouth like a victor entering a conquered town: a sweet enemy, which I was reluctant to part with. My own tongue submissively welcomed the intruder, caressing it and mingling our saliva. A delightful pastime which could only end one way. A game which filled my mouth, which was distilling the most delicious fluid within me.

That kiss intoxicated my senses and drew sighs of ecstacy from me. The first contact of mouths is, in my opinion, the most beautifully voluptuous of sensations.

We moved even closer together. My breasts were flattened almost painfully against his strong chest and my belly pressed against Michel's.

Suddenly, his hands started to move downwards, not stopping until they reached my prominent buttocks. What were they about, those impudent hands? They cupped my bottom-cheeks, then started to knead them gently. What an exquisite feeling! I could feel the heat of his hands through my dress and knickers. All of my consciousness seemed to be centred in the area which Michel's hands were caressing so expertly. Oh, how happy I felt! My

23

bottom seemed to be endowed with a life of its own at that moment! I longed to be naked, lying face down so that those hands could caress my naked bottom-cheeks. I wanted him to take complete possession of my whole body while his tongue was exploring my mouth.

How long did that kiss last? I have no idea. At last, I broke away, panting, intoxicated with sensual pleasure. No one had ever kissed me so well. As in a dream I saw Michel's face smiling at me and I heard him say, 'I'll see you tomorrow.'

Then he disappeared into the shadows.

Furtively, like a thief, I slipped into my room carefully locking the door behind me. I collapsed onto the bed, my body still trembling with desire. Hot and cold flushes ran through me. A feeling of increasing tension filled my whole being: I must do something . . .

Gently, almost unconsciously, my hands raised my skirt to my hips. The gusset of the knickers was soaking wet with female love-juice and I eased them off, then threw them across the room where they fell in a crumpled heap of blue silk on the carpet. I was now ready to seek some relief.

My fingers slid perversely between my thighs and rested upon the warm, damp fruit of love in its nest of pubic hair. How often they had performed that delightful task of relieving my unsatisfied desires! They were well-acquainted with that particular passion-fruit; they alone knew how to make it weep tears of joy.

My fingers stroked the moist flesh, but my fevered imagination transformed them into Michel's fingers: it was he who was stroking me with such expertise. The cup of pleasure, which had been brimming for

24

some time, now began to overflow. The room was filled with my sighs and moans. My half-naked body jerked in spasms of voluptuous pleasure which had been awakened by the man who would soon become my lover.

HE

What a delightful surprise! At the very moment when I was wondering how I was going to be able to bear a whole month in this place, I met, quite by chance, the most charming creature that I have ever had the good fortune to encounter. So much for my supposed rest-cure!

We met for the first time this morning in one of the village streets. I was immediately impressed by the slender elegance of the young woman, who looks much more like the kind of sophisticated coquettes one sees in the Avenue du Bois than a local girl! My word, what a lovely creature! She walked with the confident step of a mannequin and the tweed two-piece she was wearing was simple but elegant. And what lovely features! A face made for love, with an expression of innocent perversity. The make-up had been applied expertly, somewhat excessively perhaps, but I rather liked it that way. . . . A magnificent, sensual mouth, blonde hair which was obviously cared for by the best Parisian hairdressers . . . In short, she was a marvel! Who could she be? A fashionable society lady? Hum! The disturbing expression I had seen in those green eyes as she passed me in the street indicated rather a vamp! . . . A tart who'd come for a rest in the country? Perhaps, but a high-class tart, at all events!

Fascinated, I turned round and watched her. And I could see that she looked as nice from the rear as from the front. A slender, flexible back like that of a dancer, long and shapely legs sheathed in silk, and hips! . . . Hips that were calculated to put a whole regiment of lovers on a war-footing! The tight skirt did nothing to conceal two prominent, well-rounded buttocks and partly revealed the cleft which separated them as well! For a long time I stood there transfixed by so many feminine charms, the provocative sway of that womanly bottom in particular was a magnificent spectacle for a connoisseur!

For the rest of the morning I couldn't get her out of my mind and when lunch-time came I installed myself in the hotel's dining-room in the hope that she would appear. And I was not disappointed! She arrived and sat at a table almost opposite mine. What a piece of luck!

The waitress was a pretty local girl called Thérèse, who knows how to wear sheer silk stockings and apply make-up. The crafty girl has been doing everything in her power to arouse my interest in her ever since I arrived. Undoubtedly Thérèse had noticed that all my attention was concentrated on the newcomer, for she served me very brusquely at first but suddenly changed her tactics: now she brushed against me with her perfumed skirt and bent down unnecessarily low when serving me to reveal two round white breasts nestling in her corsage like two tender doves. But it was all in vain! My hands would never caress those lovely breasts. Only one woman interested me now, and that was the beautiful stranger who looked at me with a faint smile as she began to eat.

After a while, I found a pretext for speaking to her.

I learnt that, like me, she is here for a month. That piece of information strengthened my hope!

We spent some time chatting about various things, then decided to go to the village fair together. But first of all the lovely girl, whose name is Jacqueline Dambleuse, asked me to excuse her for a few moments while she went upstairs to change. She returned shortly wearing a muslin frock which was not quite so form-hugging as the two-piece, but I guessed that she was near-enough naked underneath it.

Then we went to the fair. I like the atmosphere of those little country fairs and never miss an opportunity to go to them, for I love feeling the bottoms of the local girls all dressed up in their Sunday-best. But this afternoon the behinds of the country lasses held no interest for me. All my interest was concentrated on the magnificent Jacqueline!

With a childlike enthusiasm, she wanted to have a go on the swings. As I have a horror of that particular pastime, I contented myself with watching her. It was a pleasant sight. She looked so pretty in the swing-boat, like a fragile doll in its box.

If only she would stand up though! Then the spectacle would really be worth watching!

It was as if she had read my thoughts! There she was, standing up in the swing-boat, her hands gripping the ropes. And then, as I had hoped it would, the wind suddenly whisked her skirt up! Oh, what delightful mysteries were thus revealed! Such nice thighs, so plump and white above the stocking-tops, and contrasting so nicely with the pale blue of the suspenders . . . and how elegant and tasteful the little blue knickers were!

My word, what a lovely sight! Every time the swing arrived directly above me, I could see right up Jacqueline's skirt! Her firm stomach and the mysterious region between the thighs were tightly moulded by the knickers. I could clearly see the young woman's buttocks too under the clinging blue silk.

She could see that I was staring at her. What would she do? Pull her skirt down and hold it down with her knees pressed together? That would be a pity! The dear little thing wouldn't be at all worried if she really knew what I thought, for I detest hypocrisy and would never think badly of a woman for revealing her thighs.

But she turned out to be a real sport! Jacqueline did not attempt to pull her skirt down. On the contrary she continued to let me admire her intimate charms in the most unconstrained manner.

Up, down, up down. My sensual excitement increased with the rhythm of the swing. As she passed back and forth I had alternating views of the front and back: belly, bottom, belly, bottom. There was a perverse innocence about it which charmed me.

At last, she got off the swing, blushing because of her shameless display. She gave me a shy smile, undoubtedly wondering what I thought of her.

'How about having a go on the roundabout?' I said.

She agreed with a childlike joy, clapping her hands together excitedly. What a strange creature! One moment a formidably adult woman, the next a delightful little girl.

We both mounted the same wooden horse, for only one was free. That caused Jacqueline's skirt to ride up quite high, revealing her pretty legs in their sheer silk stockings, and some bare flesh was visible too. She raised her skirt from behind in order to avoid creasing it: this meant that the only thing separating her bare bottom from the varnished wood of the horse's back was the thin silk of her knickers! How I should have loved to slip my hand under the young woman's buttocks! But I mustn't get carried away! A prospective lover must sometimes know how to proceed with patience, in order not to risk spoiling his chances.

The lovely creature leant back against me. I could feel the warmth of her body pressing against mine. Such intimate contact soon had its effect, and my virility awakened in my trousers. But I didn't want her to become aware of that.

The merry-go-round started to turn. Jacqueline laughed unaffectedly like a kid. Her blonde curls tickled my face and I could smell her perfume.

I ventured to put my arms round the young woman, cupping her breasts with my hands. They nestled there cosily and the nipples were clearly discernible. I caressed them with my fingers and felt them grow harder. Would she be offended? To be honest, she would have had a perfect right to be. A lady does not allow any Tom, Dick or Harry to paw her breasts about . . . But then, perhaps she wasn't a lady, and perhaps I was by no means the first man who had taken such liberties!

She made no attempt to stop me all the time we were on the merry-go-round. We got off it without looking at each other. I sensed that, like me, she had been aroused by the ride, which would certainly not be the last one we took together!

After taking a short stroll, we returned to the hotel. She went up the stairs in front of me, which gave me another opportunity to look at those undulating buttocks.

The corridor was deserted. Jacqueline, looking somewhat embarrassed, offered me her hand.

'I'll see you soon,' she said.

At that moment I recalled that I was to dine out with some friends. I didn't mind really. A short respite would do neither of us any harm, for we would have plenty of time to make love in the weeks to come.

However, when she realized that I wouldn't be dining here this evening, Jacqueline couldn't conceal her disappointment. An expression of sadness came into her eyes. She looked adorable: I couldn't leave her without a kiss.

Gently, I drew the lovely woman to me. She did not resist. Her beautiful, generous mouth was close to mine.

To pluck that flower . . . What a temptation! I could resist it no longer and pressed my lips to Jacqueline's. They were soft and warm and she responded ardently.

Almost immediately the dear little slut opened her lips. Since the door had been opened to me, it would have been silly on my part not to go in!

I slid my tongue into Jacqueline's mouth and encountered hers, which was soft, pointed and slippery with saliva. For a few moments I contented myself with exploring the wet, velvet delights of that open mouth.

Then I pulled her lovely body close to mine and could feel her breasts pressing against my chest. My hands caressed the young woman's back, gradually moving lower down until they reached that generous bottom which had done so much to inflame me. I became bolder: I began by stroking those round buttocks and ended up kneading them, but not hard enough to hurt her. Jacqueline sighed responsively, her perfumed breath mingling with mine. She didn't remain passive but pressed her bottom against my exploring hands, wriggling it lasciviously. I could see that she was totally submissive to my amorous desires, happy to be explored and felt. Her behind positively danced under the caressing fingers, sometimes making as if to escape by a contraction of the buttocks, but then immediately submitting again, abandoning all ideas of modesty.

But my increasing excitement made it unwise for me to continue those dangerous games. Regretfully, I drew away from her, squeezed her hand affectionately, then quickly disappeared into my room.

Jacqueline, obviously very disturbed, went into her room which is next to mine. What would she do now? She must be sitting down, or perhaps standing by the window, still quivering with unsatisfied desire. But, on the other hand, it was conceivable that such a sophisticated woman was much less moved than she appeared to be.

Suddenly, it seemed to me that a soft, plaintive sighing and moaning was coming from her room. I listened attentively, imagining a charming scene: the suggestive spectacle of a wicked little girl indulging in some solitary consolation.

But no, that was not possible! I must have been mistaken. Jacqueline couldn't be as sensual as that, surely?

II

Sunday, 13th June, 1937.

SHE

What a lovely day it's been!

When I look back on it, I still feel deeply moved by all the wonderful things that have happened, and in such a short space of time!

I woke up at ten o'clock this morning, got straight out of bed and began my ablutions. I was taking a shower when there was a knock at the door. Without stopping to dry myself, I slipped into a dressing gown and went into the bedroom to find Michel Semblier standing there, fully dressed. He smiled at my air of embarrassment, my dishevelled hair and my bare feet under the multi-coloured dressing gown.

'I do hope I'm not disturbing you!' he said, without conviction.

And since my only response was a rather stupid smile, he took me in his arms and kissed me passionately. I gave a gasp of surprise but didn't resist. I was very conscious of my naked body, still damp from the shower, under the dressing gown. The latter had come open and one of my breasts was exposed. I only noticed that when we separated, and made haste to cover it up. But not quickly enough to prevent Michel from getting a good look at it, and then an expression of lust came into his eyes.

'The weather is absolutely wonderful!' he said. 'How do you fancy a spin in the car, followed by lunch at Saint-Jean-de-Luz?'

'Oh, that would be lovely!. But I must get ready. I shan't be long, about half an hour.'

'Would you like me to help you?' said Michel jokingly. 'I'm an excellent lady's maid, you know.'

I laughingly refused his offer and pushed him towards the door.

In record time I finished washing, applied my make-up but hesitated over what to wear. At last I chose a pretty little white dress with a red belt, which was brand new and very form-hugging. I wanted to be a credit to my companion.

As little as possible under the dress. No suspender-belt: garters would hold my stockings up . . . I've got some delightful ones, embroidered with flowers. A lacy brassière to prevent my breasts from jiggling about too much. Finally, a pair of little silken knickers embroidered with yellow lace. An elegant white summer jacket and a small felt hat completed the outfit. I smiled contentedly at myself in the mirror then went downstairs to join my companion, who was waiting in the car.

Now we were driving along the road, leaving the village far behind us. Oh, the intoxicating feeling engendered by the sunshine, the space, the wind blowing in one's face! Nature was in full bloom on both sides of the road, there was a heady atmosphere of springtime and adventure in the air.

The wind hit me in the face like a brutal lover, but I didn't mind at all. I offered my face to it, breathing it in delightedly.

Beside me, Michel was concentrating on driving but he looked at me from time to time and smiled charmingly.

By now, we had arrived at the Basque coast. Pine plantations bathed in golden sunlight lined the route and, not far away, we could see the infinitely blue sea. The pretty coastal resort seemed to be dozing in the midday heat.

We had lunch on the terrace of a restaurant overlooking the sea. There were beautiful flowers everywhere. I had an excellent appetite, which had been sharpened by the fresh air and the excitement of the excursion. I ate with great relish, positively devouring everything which was set before me. Michel, on the contrary, hardly touched his food. 'He only had eyes for me,' to quote the words of a currently popular song. Under the table his feet were making advances to mine. I felt his knees pressing against my knees. I smiled indulgently. Waves of contentment washed over me . . . Everything seemed so right: the sunshine, the setting, the handsome young man sitting there with me . . . and what he was doing . . . Gradually though my sense of contentment gave way to a more intense pleasure. I became conscious of how little I was wearing under my dress and moved my bottom around voluptuously on the chair.

The liqueur which accompanied our coffee increased my state of intoxication. I felt good, so voluptuously good! I felt ready for anything, provided it was for the gratification of my senses. If Michel had rented a room then and taken me to it to make love, I wouldn't have raised any objections. It would have been a pleasure to lie naked on a bed and open my thighs to him.

But such was not the intention of my future lover.

He paid the bill and, resting his elbows on the table, leant towards me.

'The beach will be crowded and so will everywhere else here,' he said. 'Shall we move on, away from Saint-Jean-de-Luz?'

I didn't need to reply: my eyes spoke for me. It's quite amazing the influence that man has on me! My sole desire is to please him. Has he cast a spell on me?

The car now followed the road through the dunes. But we didn't go very far because we found a quiet spot which seemed ideally suited to two lovers who wanted to be on their own for a while. One could shelter from the hot sunshine in the cool shade of the pines or larches. No one would be likely to disturb us there, and we could see the sea.

We got out of the car and strolled around looking for a comfortable place to sit down. Michel had put his arm round my waist; he kissed the nape of my neck from time to time as we walked.

'Let's sit here, sweetheart,' he said. 'There's no-one about.'

He looked at the warm, golden sand which lay at our feet. We were hidden from inquisitive eyes by the dunes. In front of us was the sea: a paradise for Lovers!

As I sat down I was suddenly overcome by embarrassment: for the past hour a need to make water had been growing stronger within me. It had now reached the point where it would be impossible for me to hold out much longer!

The trouble is I'm always overwhelmed with shame at the very idea of speaking to a man about such things. This unhealthy bashfulness has caused me several disagreeable moments. A particularly painful memory is of a dinner-party where my inhibition resulted in me wetting my knickers! Certain women are like that: if they are prevented for any reason from immediately relieving themselves, they can't hold it in.

Blushing a little, I turned to my companion:

'Would you excuse me for a few moments?'

'Of course, my love,' he replied with an almost imperceptible smile.

I walked away rapidly among the dunes. At last I found the ideal place where there was a bush to protect me from inquisitive eyes. In a twinkling my knickers were lowered and I squatted down like a little village girl. Ooh, what a relief! But a feeling of uneasiness prevented me from relaxing: suppose Michel could hear my water cascading forth . . . I should die of shame!

Suddenly, a small sound from the other side of the bush convinced me that he was watching me. Scarlet with confusion, I stood up before I had really finished and hastily pulled my knickers up. Then the catastrophe occurred! My need had not been fully satisfied and I wet my knickers! What a disgrace! What would happen now?

I rejoined my companion with a disagreeable sensation of wet silk clinging to my lower regions. Oh well, too bad! What can't be cured must be endured!

Naturally, as soon as I sat down Michel put his arms around me and started to kiss me. Reclining on the warm sand, I responded ardently but kept my eyes wide open and looked up at the blue sky above us. What a wonderful moment that was! A voluptuous languor gradually took possession of me which communicated itself to the most intimate regions of my body. I was responding unrestrainedly to my lover's kisses, thrusting my slippery tongue into his mouth and pressing myself against him. I wanted to be naked, to be possessed by him on that bed of hot sand!

Michel pulled back from me a bit than started to caress my breasts through the dress. Getting bolder, he inserted his hand into the low-cut V-neckline, gently eased down one of the cups of the brassière and was soon caressing my exposed right breast . . . Emboldened even further by my lack of resistance, he next undid some of the buttons which were on the front of the dress, then eased the breast out of its prison of clothing. Michel seemed transfixed by the sight of the swelling smooth whiteness with the erect ruby nipple, which seemed to be asking to be caressed.

In no time at all Michel had exposed my other breast. Did I feel no shame at all at exposing my bosom like that to a young man I had only met the previous day? No, I felt no shame. Nor did I feel anything but pleasure when he bent forward and began to kiss it.

I could feel his warm breath on my bare flesh. How gentle it was, yet how masterful, that mouth which had taken possession of my breasts! He bestowed a thousand kisses upon them, all as light as the caress of a butterfly's wings. I felt myself melting with pleasure.

After a while, he took one of the stiff nipples into his mouth and began to suck. He ran his tongue expertly around the red pointing flesh, causing me so much pleasure that I moaned loudly. Waves of intense pleasure washed over me. The nipple seemed to grow even harder, to swell like a tiny ripening fruit. Lying there, a soft heap on the sand, I was ready for anything. How long did my boyfriend remain there absorbed in his sweet task? I have no idea. I was no longer aware of anything but sensations of pleasure running through me.

Then he turned his attention to the other breast. And when at last the young man paused for breath, red-faced and dishevelled, my whole being seemed to be concentrating in those swelling globes of flesh.

Again he kissed me, rendering me soft and trembling with voluptuousness. Michel's hands caressed my back, moving downwards until they were cupping my bottom-cheeks.

What perverse instinct prompted me to turn over at that moment and lie face-downwards in the sand? Undoubtedly, the desire for yet more caresses. My bottom is quite big and must have looked provocative under the light material of the summer dress.

Michel caressed my bare back, then moved down to those softly swelling hillocks. He gently stroked my buttocks as a man might stroke a crupper of a horse he is contemplating buying . . . A somewhat degrading thought but today I didn't mind: I had decided to be a submissive animal . . .

So when Michel's fingers moved away from my buttocks and began to explore the furrow between them, I put up only a token resistance and soon let him have his way.

'You're so beautiful,' he murmered. 'So incredibly beautiful! If only you knew how much I desire you!'

Sprawling there on the sand, I shuddered with pleasure, almost as if I had been penetrated physically. My breasts were flattened under me and had imprinted their outline in the soft sand.

Michel rested his head on my behind, gently rubbing his cheek against it, like a big amorous cat. The well-rounded plumpness obviously delighted him. Then, suddenly intoxicated by the idea of so much bare flesh so close, protected only by the thin layer of skirt and knickers, he bit me lightly upon one of my buttocks.

'Hey!' I remonstrated. 'My derrière isn't a beefsteak you know.'

'Oh come on now! I didn't hurt you! But it seems to me that you'd quite like it if I did!'

That was true; he was quite right, the wretch! Until then I had never shown the slightest disposition towards masochism, but with a partner like Michel . . .

Feeling somewhat embarrassed, I turned round and sat up, only to find myself in his arms again. Once more he was kissing me passionately. Then, while he caressed me with one hand, his other hand descended, grasped the hem of my skirt and pulled it half way up my thighs. All the time he kept kissing me, undoubtedly hoping to paralyse any feminine modesty which might thwart his designs.

But to be honest, I was so excited that I was not inclined to put up any resistance. I had had enough experience in these matters to know what was going to happen next: first the hand caressing my thighs, then moving higher until it reached the knickers . . . The knickers! Oh, goodness me! I'd quite forgotten about the little accident in the dunes! My knickers were still wet and if he touched them, Michel would laugh at me as one laughs at a dirty little girl, rather disgustedly!

Blushing furiously, I tried to push the exploring hand away.

'No, Michel, not that . . . please!'

No one could have been more deaf to my pleas. His mouth crushed itself against mine.

'Michel! My dearest!'

That bold hand was stroking the smooth flesh at the top of my thighs and moving ever onwards to the burning centre of my womanhood.

'Michel! No!'

I squeezed my thighs together with all my strength, imprisoning Michel's hand between them in a vice-like grip. But my lover was strong. He laughed as he kissed me, and continued his advance.

I struggled frantically and gasped, 'Michel, please, I beg you! Not that!'

Astonished by so much resistance, he at last withdrew. He looked at me reproachfully.

'Jacqueline, darling, why are you so bashful all of a sudden? You're a grown woman, not a child! Until now you have accepted my caresses with total abandon, a magnificent lack of hypocrisy! I thought that, like me, you were unencumbered by all those stupid prejudices which make love so needlessly complicated. You please me, I thought I pleased you. We're both free. Life is beautiful, the sky is blue, we're alone: Why have you suddenly turned cold?'

I listened to him, deeply troubled. How I should have liked to be able to answer him, to have explained!

Instead, I replied, 'Listen, Michel, please don't be cross with me. I do sincerely believe that I love you. At all events, I feel myself to be ready . . . to do whatever pleases you. But not here, please.'

And moving closer to him, I whispered boldly in his ear:

'Let's go back to the hotel.'

The car sped along, taking us back to the village. We said not a word, Michel giving all of his attention to driving while I was lost in contemplation of the passing landscape.

We were both tense and delightfully nervous, and our tenseness increased as we approached the village, for neither of us was in any doubt as to what was going to happen. We both knew that very soon, before the red sun had disappeared beyond the crest of the mountains, Michel Semblier would be my lover. I would give myself to him, naked and defenceless. He would possess all of me: my body, my thoughts, together with my heart. What a joy it is to dispose of oneself freely, to fly in the face of convention, to choose a man and to grant him what one has refused to others simply because one finds him pleasing!

I was longing for us to arrive so that I could offer myself warm and naked to my new master. My nipples hardened in anticipation, my lips were ready for his kisses.

At last we arrived! We kissed briefly in the corridor upstairs.

'My room or yours?' demanded Michel.

'Mine, in five minutes,' I replied.

Alone in my room, I undressed and quickly performed the most intimate of ablutions so that my secret femininity should be sweet-smelling and worthy of Michel.

I hastily combed my hair and applied a little rouge to my cheeks.

Then it was necessary to choose which pyjamas I should wear. There are some extremely seductive ones in my collection! I decided in favour of a pair with a black lacy semi-transparent jacket of which the trousers are in black silk, very hip-hugging, and flared at the bottom. They made me look rather tarty, but that didn't worry me! I would only be wearing them for a short time.

There was a knock at the door. It was Michel

getting impatient. I called to him to enter. He had had the good taste not to change into his pyjamas: that would have shocked me!

For a few moments we just stood there smiling rather inanely at each other. Such moments are usually a bit awkward. It seems impossible that one's dreams are going to be realized.

But what a mistake! With Michel they were realized very quickly! He sat on the edge of my single bed and pulled me down on to his knees. The warmth emanating from his thighs penetrated the thin silk covering my buttocks: an agreeable and intimate contact.

We didn't say a word. The language of kisses and caresses has no need of words! Michel buried his face between my breasts. He inhaled my perfume and seemed very excited. As for me, I could feel my nipples growing harder while my breasts seemed to swell.

He tried to take my lacy top off and I did everything possible to help him. So there I was, naked to the waist, with my snowy white breasts and smooth shoulders revealed to Michel. For a moment, he contented himself with just looking admiringly then, gripping my shoulders firmly, he began to kiss my breasts.

We fell back on the bed, locked together in a close embrace. I was finding it more and more difficult to think clearly about what was happening as my whole being was overcome by passion.

Michel was half lying on top of me. His arms were wrapped tightly around me, his mouth glued to mine in a fiercely voluptuous kiss. His body may have been heavy, but I shouldn't have minded if it had been twice as heavy, I was so happy to be embraced by those strong arms!

My new master gently eased my pyjama trousers down. The garment slipped lightly down my hips. I broke away from Michel for a moment and finished taking them off, then fell back on to the bed, completely naked now! Any modesty which I may once have possessed seemed to have disappeared completely.

He gazed at me with eloquently shining eyes. He obviously felt the excitement of the spectator when the curtain rises on a brand new play, a play in which, however, he was going to act the principal part! The look in his eyes went far beyond mere admiration. I felt so happy! I didn't think I was as beautiful as all that! His gaze wandered slowly over me, moving from my face to my painted toenails: a gaze so intense that I could almost feel it like a hand caressing me. But wherever his eyes wandered, they kept returning with a growing insistence to the very heart of my femininity, the tender portal between my thighs, with its covering of fleecy blonde hair.

I was breathing in short gasps. I truly believe that if Michel had gone on looking at me like that for a couple of more minutes, I would have had a violent orgasm without his even touching me!

'No more, Michel,' I said supplicatingly. 'I can't bear it any longer!'

Then I added very softly:

'Come!'

He rapidly divested himself of his clothes and in less than no time was lying naked beside me, enfolding me in his arms. Moaning with pleasure, I clung fiercely to that hard masculine body, pressing my belly against his, entwining my legs with his legs.

Soon Michel was lying on top of me, dominating me with his whole weight. He kissed my neck, my

43

ears, my shoulders. He was holding me so tightly clasped to him that I had difficulty in breathing.

What was I at that moment? A woman in love giving herself to the man she had chosen, or simply a wild animal seeking to attain an orgasm?

I no longer knew. My body did not belong to me, neither did my thoughts. I was ready to give everything to the man lying on top of me . . . He could do what he liked with me!

All I knew for certain was that I was in love. I loved his good looks, his intelligence and many other qualities in him which it would have been impossible for me to define at that stage. Love at first sight, that's what it was!

With any other man I would have been coquettish, a vamp . . . I would have held out for weeks . . . months even, and if in the end I had yielded, it would have been through curiosity, vice, the attraction of forbidden fruit.

But how different it was with Michel! Hardly had I met him yesterday morning when a secret voice whispered to me that I should be his docile slave. If he had said, 'Let us wait for two years before we become lovers,' I would have waited gladly, only too pleased to obey him. Instead, he wanted me straight away so, without remorse, without false shame, I gave myself to him on the second day of our acquaintance, like a whore . . . It seems to me that that is what they call love.

My thoughts were in a sweet but gentle state of turmoil, entirely dominated by sensual pleasure.

A tender look from Michel, a knee firmly insinuating itself between mine . . . I understood and without attempting to resist, spread my thighs wide apart, offering the supreme gift to him. For a brief moment he knelt there contemplating what was his to take, then a few gentle kisses dispelled that anguish which a woman always feels when she is about to be possessed for the first time.

Michel's body lay against mine and I felt something hot and hard pressing against my belly. Then his fingers started to play with my sex, separating the lips, stroking skilfully.

Lying there with closed eyes and open mouth, I revelled in the sweet sensations of total self-abnegation which were engulfing me.

The fingers left me and were immediately replaced by his stiff weapon which slipped in quite easily because I was so wet. I moaned ecstatically and pushed forward to welcome the sweet invader. What a wonderful moment when that hot hard length penetrates one for the first time, stretching one's silken sheath, brooking no opposition!

The man crouching between my thighs now began to move in and out in a steady rhythm. He was red in the face and gasping, my sturdy rider, as he rode me, his docile mount.

I adapted myself to the rhythm, moving my bottom to meet the thrusting organ.

I too was gasping with pleasure, digging my painted nails into the young man's back and clasping him to me as if I never wanted to let him go again. At each thrust he seemed to penetrate even deeper. His stiff weapon moved relentlessly back and forth inside me.

I looked up into his passion-contorted face and said, 'Come, Michel. I'm ready for you, my love, my sweetheart! Come now!'

My lover's response was to increase the speed and urgency of his thrusts. We were both gasping loudly as we strove together to attain the supreme release.

Then I reached my peak, bathing the organ inside me with a hot flood of female lust. Michel went rigid and he too started to come, inundating me with his fluid, a soothing balm pouring into the open wound of pleasure. Welcome intoxicating and beneficent semen! Fill my love-sheath to overflowing with your warm, odorous presence!

At last it was over . . . Michel collapsed beside me, burying his face in the soft hollow of my neck. A few spasms still ran through me and I missed that lovely stiff weapon which had just been withdrawn. I could feel Michel's breath caressing my neck.

The room was calm and silent. I lay on my back watching the filtered sunlight on the ceiling: filtered because the curtains were drawn. How pleasing they are, those moments of peaceful relaxation which follow the storms of love!

It was not only my body which I had given to Michel Semblier: I had also given him my heart!

HE

What a strange and delightful creature Jacqueline Dambleuse is! I honestly think it wouldn't take much to make me fall in love with her!

What a good thing that I don't believe in love! I say what a good thing because, while respecting that most beautiful of all sentiments, it seems to me that a certain mistrust is justified because of all the calamities it has so often led to. So if I affirm that I no longer believe in love, that's because I don't want it to fall on my head some day!

But there is no denying that Jacqueline pleases me. There is in her a strange mixture of woman of the world and lady of easy virtue which I have never encountered previously. Obviously she is very sophisticated and would be quite at ease in the best society. Sometimes too she can be as bashful as a little girl . . . Yet without really knowing me, she gave herself to me today with an openness and abandonment which is hard to explain. Is she a tart? I don't really think so. There is something too refined, too distinguished about her for that! At no time have I noticed in her any of those shocking details which betray the professional or the gold-digger. No, she made love to me for the sheer pleasure of it, healthily and honestly . . . Perhaps too because she has fallen in love with me. I'm not really fatuous enough to believe that . . . but who knows?

At all events, one thing is certain: a perfect physical harmony reigns between us, a harmony such as I have never previously experienced with any other woman. Our bodies please each other, understand each other and get on admirably well together.

Let us recapitulate the events of the day . . . Quite early this morning I went to Jacqueline's room to suggest that we should go for a drive. When I entered, she was wearing nothing but a light bath-robe which did little to conceal the magnificent shape of her body. Not knowing quite what to say and feeling somewhat embarrassed because I had entered without being invited, I decided to act boldly: I took the young woman in my arms and kissed her passionately. She was still damp from the shower and smelt good.

In her confusion, Jacqueline has let the bath-robe fall open, giving me a glimpse of two beautifully-formed white breasts with very red nipples . . . Only a glimpse, alas, for she saw me looking at them and

47

hastily drew the robe together, blushing furiously. I was very excited; what I had seen made me want to discover more hidden charms! But, I reminded myself, a bit of patience often pays big dividends. A nice lunch on a terrace overlooking the sea, a few sweet words murmured in her ear, and Jacqueline would be mine. I would take the pretty little slut in the sand, among the dunes.

Half an hour later we were bowling along in my car. She looked more ravishing that ever with her lovely blonde hair and her rather over-applied make-up. I liked the elegant white outfit she was wearing too, which was offset nicely by a red brooch, red belt and matching shoes.

I will pass rapidly over our drive and the meal which followed it. My companion was very vivacious, very joyful. When she looked at me, her big green eyes were full of affection, then she would suddenly lower those long eyelashes.

We fled from Saint-Jean-de-Luz and its fashionable crowds. I pretended not to know where we were going, but I knew allright. We were heading for a quiet spot in the dunes where no one would be able to see us. At about the same time last year, I had taken a charming little Brazilian woman there and we had made love on the warm sand without anyone to see us but the birds. You might think that it's not a very nice thing to do to take Jacqueline to the same place, but men often get a lot of pleasure from such mild indecencies.

We had now arrived at that quiet spot. Before sitting down, Jacqueline asked me to excuse her for a few moments, and she walked off, her hips swaying indolently. I looked at those generous buttocks, which the thin skirt did little to conceal, and was immediately aroused.

I had a sudden urge to follow the young woman, to spy upon her while she performed a most intimate function. I know, I should be ashamed of myself! But my sensuality overcame my sense of decorum and I followed her stealthily, like a Sioux on the warpath.

Jacqueline walked along until she came to a clump of bushes then, thinking that no one could see her, she hitched up her skirt and pulled down her knickers. What a pleasant sight to see a grown woman behaving just like a little girl! I could never get tired of such a spectacle, and now I had a lovely view from the crest of the dune behind which I was hiding.

She was wearing white knickers! I had thought they would be pink. But what does the colour matter? The important thing is that the lady was pulling them down! The delicate garment hung round her ankles. Then, holding her skirt up, the young woman squatted down. The sound of water gushing forth was borne to me on the wind blowing across the dunes.

But I was suddenly overcome by a sense of shame. What an odious thing for someone who considered himself a gentleman to be doing! Here was a ravishing young woman who had shown me nothing but kindness and who would undoubtedly soon become my mistress; why did I need to spy on her like that, to indulge in such an unhealthy form of pleasure?

I made as if to move away, but Jacqueline must have heard me. She jumped up quickly, pulling her knickers up and her skirt down in record time. She looked very anxious, poor little thing! If she found out about my shameful behaviour, it would be all over between us before we had even started.

At last we were sitting side by side on the sand. We

kissed tenderly. Never have I received such pleasure from a woman's lips! Jacqueline's mouth was delightfully soft and yielding and her breath was sweet. I could feel her firm breasts pressing against my chest, which awoke a strong desire in me to see them. It didn't take me long to unfasten her corsage and expose one of them, for Jacqueline put up no resistance.

What a lovely breast it was: gently swelling smooth whiteness, with a faint tracery of blue veins and crowned with a bright red nipple! A pretty bosom is always a joy to see. That breast was so perfect that it fascinated me, filled me with admiration. If this first glimpse of beauty was anything to go on, undressing Jacqueline was going to be a uniquely rewarding experience!

It was not long before I uncovered the young woman's other breast. I stroked them and felt them and played with the prominent nipples.

The temptation was too great! I bent down, took one of those raspberries into my mouth and started to suck and tongue it. Jacqueline whimpered with pleasure, the little love-fruit hardened and seemed to grow larger. I felt a certain part of myself growing hard as well and continued with my sensual ministrations. From time to time the young woman tried to push me away, but without much conviction. I inhaled the subtle perfume emanating from her warm flesh, which aroused me even more.

At length, in order to get her breath, the lovely girl broke away, rolling over onto her belly on the sand. She looked extremely enticing lying there in front of me. The thin summer dress was very revealing and her bottom was clearly outlined by the clinging material. Those round buttocks looked so inviting that it was impossible for me to resist the desire to stroke them. I felt her quiver when I touched her.

My desire was increasing in intensity: the rod of flesh between my thighs was stiff and throbbing.

I laid my head on those soft buttocks, feeling the warmth of the young woman's body through the thin material. The thought of those naked bottom-cheeks so close to me nearly sent me crazy with lust; it was impossible to resist the sudden impulse which overwhelmed me: I bit them, one after the other, but not hard enough to really hurt.

Then we were kissing again, hard and passionately. Now was the moment to be decisive! As unobtrusively as possible, I placed a hand on my companion's knee . . . such a smooth, round knee! Then gradually I started to move upwards, all the while kissing her and stroking her thigh. The moment when one is about to explore the most intimate secrets of a woman for the first time is always maddeningly exciting!

However, Jacqueline was being less cooperative than when I had been feeling her breasts. She halted my advance by imprisoning my hand between her thighs – those thighs which are so warm, so incredibly soft to the touch! I let things rest there for a moment in order to lull the pretty creature into a false sense of security. Then I resumed the attack.

Not far to go now! My fingers had already attained the lacy edge of the little white knickers. Now they had reached their goal: I could feel the hairy mound in its silken prison. She was positively wringing wet with desire. That seemed to me to be an excellent sign.

But suddenly Jacqueline pushed me away quite determinedly. It seemed a bit late in the day to start playing the prude!

She was quite inflexible now . . . All my efforts were in vain! She refused to let me take any more liberties. I couldn't understand this sudden change of attitude, this transformation from willing acceptance to frigid resistance. Was it possible that Jacqueline was in reality one of those nasty little tarts who will permit a man every favour except the ultimate one?

My vanity was wounded, my desires unsatisfied. I tried to reason with her, to make her change her mind. But it was she who changed my mind, for she suddenly bent forward and whispered in my ear that if we went back to the hotel . . .

Suddenly all my optimism returned; we drove back to the hotel at top speed. Her apologetic and submissive attitude made me feel as if she were my slave to do as I liked with!

Alone in my room, I smoked a cigarette to try to calm my impatience. I could hear Jacqueline moving about on the other side of the wall: the sound of water running, the faint rustle of clothes being removed. My excitement increased, my heart beat faster. I thought I was more blasé, and here I was like a college boy about to commit his first sin!

When she opened the door in response to my discreet knock a few moments later, she was wearing very suggestive pyjamas, her cheeks were flushed and a heady perfume emanated from her lovely body. In spite of my wide experience with many women, I realized that Jacqueline was quite exceptional. I intended to pay a more than adequate tribute to such charms!

The sweet girl came into my arms and we lay down together on the bed. After a few caresses interspersed with passionate kisses, she slipped out of those enticing pyjamas. There she was, splendidly naked, revealing her slender body with its generous curves to me, gazing up at me with the eyes of a frightened doe. I have noticed that all women, even the most experienced, have the expression of a girl in their eyes when they give themselves to a lover for the first time.

I gazed wonderingly at her nude form, drinking my fill of those charms, especially the fleece of fair pubic hair. I looked so intently that she was moved to exclaim:

'Your eyes! . . . They're killing me!'

Adorable creature! My eyes will soon be replaced by my mouth, my hands, my sex which will take turns in possessing you. A lover can never be just one single phenomenon: there is the lover's face, the lover's lips, the lover's words, the lover's regard, the lover's caress . . . and it is only when each of these forces has acted, one after the other, that they combine in the solemn moment of possession.

Kisses. An ocean of kisses! I pressed my lips to Jacqueline's warm perfumed body. Her skin smelt of the springtime, of jasmine. Never before had I encountered a woman who aroused my sensuality to such a degree! I couldn't get enough of her!

But there would be other nights, many other nights. The main thing now was this first act of love. The hors-d'oeuvres would come later.

I raised myself above her and insinuated my body between the young woman's open thighs. The gentle victim offered herself to me without reserve.

I felt my rigid weapon penetrate the wet, burning centre of Jacqueline's femininity. Her pale face was contracted with voluptuousness and she gave a loud gasp when she felt her love-sheath being invaded and stretched.

As I moved in and out, my testicles beating a steady

53

rhythm on the girl's bottom, she continued to gasp and moan. There is nothing more stimulating when a man is possessing a woman that to hear her making such sounds, which are a song of love revealing her feelings of submission to the male.

The cult of love, eternal gestures, unchanging and grandiose ritual . . . Whether it takes place in an anonymous hotel room or in a palace, on a sordid pallet or a prince's bed, the coupling of two naked bodies is always moving and worthy of respect. At that moment all sense of social class is abolished: a man taking a woman becomes a legendary male, his sweetheart becomes a goddess of love: this is the nobility of sensuality.

What is Jacqueline Dambleuse? A gold-digger, a tart, an adventuress? What does it matter? Jacqueline Dambleuse at that precise moment was a tall, naked girl with dishevelled hair who cried aloud with joy as I inundated her with my virile liquid.

How magnificent she was in the throes of passion! What a pity that I no longer believe in love!

III

Thursday, 17th June, 1937.
SHE

The love which was born in my heart and my body last Sunday, that marvellous Sunday, has followed an ascending curve since then. For four nights, four memorable nights, Michel has been my lover. For four sunny, laughter-filled days we have done what all lovers do: we have transformed every moment, every incident of daily life, no matter how banal, and made it into something special with our love.

I no longer accord even the briefest thought to the past. It seems to me that my life is just beginning. I who have always been disappointed, dissatisfied, have at last found in my new lover's arms that joy, the sense of physical well-being which I sought so long in vain.

So perfect is the harmony which reigns between us that we have not once been tempted to complicate it with cerebral or vicious games. In the course of these four nights we have made love healthily, normally, and every time seemed like the first time.

I do not believe that a woman's body is some sort of musical instrument which a skilful lover can play with impunity. Her psycho-sensual organization is

55

extremely delicate and sensitive and a clumsy lover could wreak havoc with it.

Michel understood this. He bided his time with great patience before initiating me to forbidden pleasures. I am grateful to him for his delicate approach. Too much haste in matters of perversion can shock a woman's sensibility and nip a blooming relationship in the bud.

And yet, in spite of the sweetness of our union, I don't know whether Michel really loves me. He desires me, there's no doubt about that. He lusts after my body, possesses it with the greatest possible pleasure, but never once has he revealed his innermost feelings to me. Neither of us has yet broached the question of what is going to happen when our holiday comes to an end.

And sometimes I am overcome with anxiety. If Michel were to grow tired of me . . . If he considers me simply as a passing fancy, an instrument of pleasure to liven up his stay in the country. If he were to break off the relationship as soon as we return to Paris . . .

I dare not reveal these fears to my lover. I do not wish to influence his decision in any way . . . He must make up his own mind whether to make me the happiest of women . . . or the most miserable.

Perhaps the young man is waiting for me to make the first bold move, the revelation of a sensual skill which he thinks I am concealing? There are certain moments, it is true, when a desire to show myself to be perverse, refined, vicious takes possession of me . . . but then I am afraid that by suddenly displaying a courtesan's talents, I might destroy whatever good opinion he has formed of me.

This evening during dinner Michel had a strange

56

expression on his face. His eyes had a brilliant, feverish appearance, he kept giving me sly glances but when I looked at him, he avoided meeting my eyes. Yet I was aware that he was looking at me very insistently, mentally undressing me as it were, and I found that disturbing. I had the impression then that Michel had become a different man!

But surely that was stupid! Wasn't I just letting my imagination run away with me?

We went up to my room. Until then, Michel had not been in the habit of joining me until I had undressed, but now he insisted upon coming in straight away.

'Come on, darling,' he whispered. 'I want to undress you myself tonight.'

He pulled me to him and after a passionate kiss, started to undress me. I smiled as I felt his clumsy fingers fiddling with the fastening of my dress. At length he succeeded and the dress fell in a dainty corolla at my feet. I stepped out of it. All I was wearing now was a pink silk brassière and matching knickers. Michel gazed at me with delight. He pulled me on to his knees and we sat there like that for some time while he kissed and caressed me. He seemed enchanted with everything which had been revealed to him.

'We haven't finished yet, darling,' I said after a while. 'You're not going to put me to bed in my knickers, are you?'

Smiling, he made me stand up, then pulled the dainty garment down until it was draped round my feet. I stepped out of it. He bent down, picked up the knickers, which were still warm from my body, then raising them to his lips, he kissed the crotch and sniffed it.

'What a nasty man you are! You ought to be ashamed of yourself!' I exclaimed, but the playful tone of my voice belied the seriousness of the words.

'I'm not ashamed,' he replied. 'There's nothing shameful about breathing in the odour of a beautiful woman. It's a part of you that I'm sniffing.'

Nevertheless, I was rather shocked.

'I can't see what satisfation you can get from what is, after all, just a wretched loin-cloth!'

'Ah, but that's because you're not a man!' he replied with an ironical smile. 'To me it's not just "a wretched loin-cloth." I've always had a weakness for ladies' knickers . . .'

'Well I'd be obliged if, in future, you would not do such things in front of me. I'd rather not know about that, or any other perversions which give you cheap thrills!'

Michel just laughed at my shrill tone of anger.

'You entirely misunderstand me, dearest!' he said. 'These knickers aren't just an anonymous object. They are a symbol of you, of your beloved body. What could be more charming than this fragile piece of silk, impregnated with the secret odours of your femininity? It is no longer just any old lingerie, because you have communicated some of your life, your warmth, your perfume to it! To think that this lace has caressed your bare thighs thousands of times, that this silk has caressed your dear little love-nest . . . Isn't that wonderful? Can you blame me for being a bit jealous of this privileged garment which is next to your most secret parts all day long?'

'Please, Michel! You're embarrassing me,' I said.

But my lover was not listening to me: he had once again plunged his face into the pink silk and was

58

delightedly inhaling the odours which emanated from it.

'This is you,' he murmured. 'The mystery of your body, your most secret juices . . .'

'Michel, *please*, I beg you!'

Regretfully, the young man at last threw the fragile garment into a corner of the room.

'Look, Jacqueline,' he said, turning to me with a smile, 'don't get the wrong idea about me. I'm not some kind of pervert. Just because I like the casket, that doesn't preclude me from liking the jewel which it contains even more! And in this case, as you well know, the jewel is your body.'

During this conversation, I had been lying on the bed, completely nude. Now Michel undressed and lay down beside me. He immediately began to kiss me with the most intense passion.

My nipples hardened at the touch of Michel's lips. But he soon abandoned them and turned his attention to my belly, pressing his mouth to the soft warm skin. It was a most agreeable sensation and I did not attempt to restrain him but just lay back, savouring the feel of those lips. For a while, he lingered over the little conch formed by my navel, then he moved downwards. I began to understand what the young man had in mind! And to think that I had so recently been congratulating myself on the *purity* of our love! But, of course, such things cannot last!

Michel pushed my thighs apart and slid between them. Now his face was very close to the sex, with its covering of coarse fair hair. I could feel his breath on my most intimate femininity.

Then that loving mouth started to kiss the hairy mound and to press itself against the sex-lips as well. I lay back, so completely overwhelmed by ecstatic feelings that I could not think of objecting to this new turn which our relationship had taken.

What a tempting serpent it was, that agile tongue which slid almost imperceptibly into my warm love-slit! With what perfidious skill it explored the very depths of me, moving up and down, in and out, then lingering lovingly over the clitoris!

My desire exacerbated to the highest point, I arched my back, my bottom wriggled frantically.

'Dearest . . . Darling Michel!' I gasped. 'That's lovely! Please don't stop!'

My hands grasped the young man's head as if I were afraid he would withdraw. Then, as the pleasure increased in intensity, a sudden feeling of shame overcame me and I endeavoured to push him away.

But it was a vain effort. He seemed to be glued to me, to that luscious fruit which was filling that sucking mouth with its juice; for Michel was sucking insatiably now! Time seemed to stand still. His tongue and lips seemed to have become an integral part of my burning sex!

At length I came, filling my lover's mouth with the warm effusion of my pleasure, and Michel went on sucking until he had taken all I had to give.

For some time after that I just lay there on the bed, completely exhausted. Michel, lying beside me, looked at me with a tender expression on his face.

Then he told me what he wanted me to do, saying that every woman who really loved her man was willing to do that for him. I hesitated however. It seemed to me that only a prostitute would do such a thing . . . or, as he said, a woman who really loved a man. With my previous lovers I had always been very reluctant to perform what still seemed to me to be a degrading task. But there, I had never really loved any of them as I love Michel.

My lover's organ was victoriously erect; it seemed to me to be staring up at me expectantly. After all, what better way was there of proving my love for him?

I started to move down towards the foot of the bed, all the while kissing Michel's hairy torso to hide my confusion.

When I reached his belly I stopped and looked at the rigid weapon, which stared back at me insolently then, holding it gently in my fingers, I kissed it. But at that moment shyness overcame me, and it seemed impossible for me to proceed further. Michel, disappointed by my hesitation, whispered a few words of encouragement, then I planted another kiss upon the shaft which still throbbed in my fingers.

Would it be possible for me to find the courage to do what Michel desired? I bent down and gave the fearsome yet beautiful object a few more kisses in order to familiarize myself with it.

My timidity was gradually disappearing however. I began to lick it, running my tongue up the entire length: doing that filled me with a strange sense of joy and my scruples disappeared completely. After a while, I took the swollen purple tip of the organ into my mouth and started to suck it gently. An intoxicating sense of exhilaration ran through me, a feeling of the absolute *rightness* of what was happening. I was no longer a wealthy lady, an elegant Parisian mannequin: I was just a naked female giving pleasure to the man I loved!

The way Michel writhed and gasped there on the bed showed how much he appreciated my efforts to please him. How simple it was! What a fuss I had made about nothing! I no longer had any idea in my mind save that of giving the maximum pleasure to my lover, of satisfying him completely.

Crouching between his thighs, I sucked him without restraint, my head constantly bobbing up and down. His staff quivered and seemed to swell to an even greater size. Then, gently but firmly, he pulled me off him just as the climax came. Long jets of greyish-white odorous liquid spurted out, landing on his chest and stomach. I had done what he wanted me to do; in fact, judging by the contented look on Michel's face, I had done it well! I felt both proud and confused.

We lay side by side on the bed, quietly enjoying the aftermath of love, resting our weary bodies.

But I could not sleep. Lying there in the darkness, I went back over what had happened.

Vice had now appeared to trouble the pure waters of our love. Was that a good or bad thing? I still can't answer that question. In any case, there was no need for me to feel ashamed . . . Yet I couldn't help wondering if my lover had not begun to despise me a little . . .

HE

Little Jacqueline has revealed another aspect of herself to me. Until this latest incident, I desired her simply, without any cerebral complications, but often wondered what lay behind her innocent smiles and ladylike reserve.

I think I have already mentioned the strange contrasts which sometimes manifest themselves in this young woman. An artless girl who had freed herself from all prejudices? Perverse? Licentious? She is all these things, yet words are so inadequate to describe her!

At first, I was in a bit of a quandary: should I just let our relationship take its natural course? Or should I, on the contrary, initiate the young woman into the complex art of forbidden caresses?

Well, in the end, Jacqueline turned out to be a lot less artless than she appeared to be. In fact, she knows quite a lot, and has just proved it. Yet there is something constrained and timid in her caresses which perplexes me.

There's no denying that when I entered her room tonight, it was my intention to introduce something new into our relationship. Which does not mean that normal love-making with this young woman no longer appealed to me, quite the contrary! But I was curious to see how far she would go.

I began by undressing her, a charming task, which would be boring for a lady's maid but delightful for a lover!

Without her frock, Jacqueling looked even more exquisite than when she was dressed and even more exciting than when she was naked. She wore extremely elegant lingerie, which revealed far more of the lovely lady's charms than it concealed!

She walked around the room wearing only a pair of pink silk knickers and matching brassière and my organ stood up in honour of so much charm. Her knickers were very brief and tight, like a second skin. From behind one could clearly see her plump bottom-cheeks, while in front the slit of the sex was unequivocally outlined.

Immediately a strange, intense desire took possession of me. I made her take the knickers off, then raising them to my lips, I kissed them, heedless

of what she might think of me for doing such a thing!
I inhaled the subtle aroma that emanated from the
fragile silk, in which Jacqueline's perfume mingled
with a more personal odour.

She seemed shocked, or at least very surprised by
this unusual form of veneration. Then I tried to
explain to her that this was not a perversion but the
act of a deeply-smitten lover. Did she understand? I
doubt it. Yet as I was speaking, Jacqueline's eyes had
a strange expression in them and her cheeks were
quite flushed. She didn't understand but she found
what I was saying exciting, that was certain.

At length my pretty mistress was naked. How lovely
that nude body looked, with its elegant, voluptuous
curves!

When I joined her on the bed, it was not my intention to have normal intercourse but rather to pay a
precise homage to the young woman's femininity.
After a few caresses and whispered endearments, I
slid down and started to kiss her stomach, then it was
not long before I was pressing my lips to the lips of
that other mouth between Jacqueline's thighs, which
was covered by a fleece of fair pubic hair.

A heady aroma emanated from that region: it was
made up of jasmine, the perfume she always uses, and
other more intimate odours which were powerfully
stimulating to the senses. No words are adequate to
describe that subtle animal odour which emanates
from a woman's femininity or from under her arms.
For a lover, no perfume is more intoxicating, more
evocative of the Eternal Feminine.

During the next few moments I did nothing but
kiss Jacqueline's sex-lips and the fleecy hair which
protected them. Then I used my fingers to separate
them and started to kiss and tongue the pretty pink

orifice which was thus revealed to me: it seemed to taste of springtime, of youth. I used my mouth with all the skill which a long experience has given me.

The young woman arched her back and moaned with pleasure. She ran her fingers through my hair, while her bottom jerked spasmodically.

I thrust my tongue even deeper into the orifice. A marvellous savour filled my mouth, arousing me even further. Jacqueline's sex-lips gaped open, the warm velvety lining of the vagina started to contract as the moment of orgasm approached.

Then she came, gasping and groaning, filling my mouth with her juices as she spent copiously.

The poor girl was so exhausted by what had happened that for quite some time she lay there almost without consciousness.

During this time I just lay beside her, contemplating her pretty face, which was now pale and undone as a result of so much voluptuous feeling. The eyes were closed, with dark circles round them, the lips slightly parted, the hair was pleasingly dishevelled, and in all that there was something subtle, a fragility, which moved me.

Was I falling in love with the little lady? In love with her body perhaps . . . but as for the rest? I should certainly hope not!

But as Jacqueline seemed to have recovered now, it occurred to me that it would be nice if she were to do for me what I had just done for her, so I told her so. She didn't refuse outright, but did look a bit taken aback. She looked at me pensively for a few moments, then disappeared under the sheet and I felt her warm lips kissing my belly.

It was a delightful sensation and before long my weapon stiffened in anticipatory excitement.

However, it took her quite some time to make up her mind to go any further. Shyness? Lack of enthusiasm? Panic at the idea of taking such a big stiff organ into her mouth? I really don't know. This lovely lady is something of an enigma – so much modesty allied to so much boldness!

But suddenly her warm wet mouth engulfed me and started to suck with an expertise which I found somewhat disconcerting. I should have preferred a little more restraint, even a bit of clumsiness. So she obviously means much more to me than I realized!

That mouth continued to suck the rigid weapon skilfully, sensually. But I couldn't seem to relax and enjoy myself fully. A sort of embarrassment (yes, that is the right word) was acting as a brake to my pleasure.

It was very strange! Quite incomprehensible! I, who have always appreciated erotic skill in my mistresses, was taken aback, disappointed to find it in Jacqueline!

But perhaps, upon reflection, it is not so incomprehensible after all: I should have liked to consider her as an inexperienced girl and to have had the pleasure of gradually initiating her to new caresses, of forming her . . . And then this sudden, disappointing revelation of perversity, so reminiscent of the other women I had known!

However, it suddenly occurred to me that to let such scruples spoil my pleasure would be ridiculous. I would be wiser to accept Jacqueline as she was and just lie back and enjoy the sweet sensations her mouth was giving me.

What right had I to complain? In this little place in the back of beyond, I had found a delightful mistress who had livened up my holiday wonderfully.

When our month was up and we found ourselves

back in Paris, I would undoubtedly grow tired of
her . . . But, in the meantime . . .

IV

Saturday, 19th June, 1937
SHE

I feel ashamed, delightfully ashamed of myself! I have arrived at that stage of love when one accepts vice as inevitable, when one no longer sees its ugliness, considering it as simply another means of expressing the intensity of one's passion.

The day before yesterday I was still afraid of being despised if I surrendered myself too completely to sensual pleasure. But today that reticence has been superseded by a kind of joyful intoxication, a total abnegation of modesty. An intense sensuality has taken possession of my entire being: I want to give myself to my lover without any reservations so that we can do what we like to the point of exhaustion, to roll with him in the glorious mire of perversion!

Things which once appeared shameful, forbidden, now seem wonderfully exciting expressions of our passion. Such is the magic power of love that embellishes, that gilds the basest things, as the sun gilds and embellishes the mud upon which it sometimes shines.

Am I the same woman now? The same woman who, a few days ago, contemplated her naked image in the mirror with a sentiment of such exclusiveness, who dessed in silken underwear for *her* pleasure?

Don't misunderstand me: I did want a lover, but in my mind I pictured such a lover as being the docile instrument of my pleasure, the servant of my desires.

Well, the lover has appeared, but he is far from being any kind of servant. On the other hand, he is *everything* for me: all I want is to belong to him completely and absolutely, even to the point of considering vice as a virtue, if that is what he wants.

Yesterday we had lunch in a little mountain chalet which has been transformed into an inn. We had a wonderful view over the valley and the silvery tinkling of the little bells which the livestock wear round their necks was wafted to us on the breeze. The meal was a simple, healthy one, accompanied by a local wine that went straight to the head. A plump country lass with apple-red cheeks served us, smiling knowingly as she did so.

When one is close to nature, one should behave naturally. Michel realized this and slipped his arm round my waist, then his hand moved down a bit and he started to feel my bottom. The fact that the waitress might come back at any second excited both of us a great deal. We kissed passionately and Michel's tongue explored my mouth. Our kisses tasted of white cheese and smoked ham. Happiness flooded through me!

Then the audacious man started to pull my skirt up! I felt too euphoric even to think of resisting and soon found myself with my skirt up round my waist! It must be admitted that I had slightly raised my bottom at the crucial moment to facilitate this operation. The straw which covered the seat of the rustic chair felt rough and uncomfortable but, to be honest, the sensation was not entirely disagreeable.

Now Michel's hand was busy again. It had insinuated itself right under me, forming a sort of cushion between my bottom and the straw seat. That would have been all right, but one of his fingers worked its way into the interstice between my bottom-cheeks and boldly started to tickle the most secret orifice! Dear Michel! He's incorrigible! I wasn't sure that I really liked that sort of thing though; the possibility that the waitress might come back began to worry me too.

In the end, I couldn't stand it any more and begged him to stop:

'Please, no more darling!'

Michel looked at me. He was very red in the face and his eyes were shining. A few days ago, such behaviour on his part would have frightened or disgusted me. Today, I couldn't help giving him a conspiratorial smile which, under the circumstances, was not a very ladylike thing to do!

'Shall we ask if we can have a room, darling?' he whispered.

I spluttered with laughter and he read my agreement in my eyes. Michel spoke to the waitress, who was also bubbling with laughter.

A few minutes later, we found ourselves alone in a rustic bedroom whose ceiling was so low that we were afraid of bumping our heads. Through an open window a green mountain slope was visible, which was covered with white cows. Three sprigs of lavender stood in a pot of water on the dressing-table.

As for the bed! . . . What a wonderful place to make love, country-style! It was so big and so high, with fresh linen sheets covered with an enormous red eiderdown.

Michel seemed enchanted. He sat me on his knees and undressed me like a precious doll. My corsage flew across the room, followed by a tweed skirt, pink knickers, stockings and finally my slip. There I was, naked but not blushing: the simple rustic atmosphere made me feel bold, self-confident.

I told my lover that I should like to undress him. Removing his jacket was easy enough, then I made the young man sit on my knees and set about taking his trousers off. But the fly gave me quite a lot of trouble. My fingers wrestled clumsily with the buttons, taking some considerable time to get them all undone. Then, suddenly, it seemed to me that the front of Michel's trousers was growing . . . It was rapidly swelling up to quite extraordinary dimensions!

Delightedly I plunged my hand into the open fly to feel for myself the miracle of growth which my fumbling fingers had produced and brought the fine upstanding weapon out into the broad light of day where I could admire it. How tempting it looked! I couldn't resist bending down and giving that fine staff a loving kiss.

'If you want to do that, we'd better lie down, darling,' said Michel with an embarrassed laugh.

He was right, of course: we should go to bed. I hastily finished undressing him and, casting an admiring glance at my lover's body, I lay down on the bed, positively trembling with desire. Michel joined me immediately and embraced me. We clung to each other under the stifling weight of the red eiderdown. In that overheated bed our bodies were soon damp with perspiration. But the beneficial heat seemed to weld our bodies together. I love a man's sweat: I sniff it with wide-open nostrils, joyfully impregnating myself with it. Nothing arouses me more than to lie with my nose buried in a lover's armpit, intoxicating myself with that animal odour!

I could feel my wet, slippery breasts crushed against Michel's hairy chest.

But then I became aware of his hot, stiff organ pressing against me and which would soon be buried deep inside me.

There was something marvellously decadent in the heat of that summer afternoon. A pleasantly stifling, heavy sensation which encouraged my lewd impulses.

Suddenly, an overwhelming desire to have Michel's virility in my mouth took possession of me. I dived under the cover and descended into the warm obscurity in search of his rigid flesh. I began by kissing his stomach and the rough pubic hairs at its base. I was now in an inverse position relative to Michel: my face was close to his abdomen, his head was between my thighs. For a few moments I licked the quivering column of flesh and he encouraged me with a few words of endearment. Then I took the swollen tip of the organ into my mouth and gently started to tongue it, nearly driving him crazy with the sensations this caused him to feel.

I was so aroused by now that spasms of excitement were rippling through my belly, my femininity was melting with desire.

But what was this? Michel had thrust his face between my wide-spread thighs, then I felt his fingers parting the sex-lips and his warm, slippery tongue penetrating me!

The resulting sensations were so intense that they caused me to stop sucking for a moment, but only or a moment! My head was soon bobbing up and down again as I took Michel's entire length into my mouth. It was not long before a sort of rhythm established itself between us, a kind of sensual morse-code. Every time the young man's tongue explored my love-nest,

72

my lips responded by sliding along his length. It was absolutely marvellous!

Until then, the claims which had been made for the efficacity of this double kiss, popularly designated by a number very close to seventy, had always seemed to me to be exaggerated. Now, for the first time, I was discovering the intense pleasure which can be derived from such a practice, when it is done with sensitivity.

It was absolutely stifling under the bedclothes, but that didn't bother me. On the contrary, it seemed to increase the intensity of my pleasure.

Clinging to Michel's body, my head between his thighs, hair dishevelled, I sucked avidly. Although my jaws were beginning to ache with the strain of so much effort, I kept sucking, sucking, sucking. It seemed to me that I no longer had just one tongue but a thousand tongues, all of them rapid and agile, exploring every inch of the rampant organ filling my mouth.

At the same time, another tongue was exploring the very depths of me, moving around in the pink, glistening orifice which I was offering to it.

We were becoming more and more excited, drawing nearer and nearer to the climax. My head was bobbing up and down furiously, then suddenly the moment of orgasm was upon us: I overflowed into Michel's mouth, while my own mouth was filled with his copious emission. We had ceased to be human-beings and had become two rutting animals whose only aim was to drain the cup of pleasure to the very dregs!

Soaked with perspiration, trembling all over, I extricated myself from under the bedclothes and lay down beside Michel. I breathed in great lungfuls of the fresh air which was coming from the open window. How good it felt after being deprived of it for so long!

Calm silence reigned in the bedroom after our recent storm of passion. I cuddled up to Michel like the sated little animal I was and fell asleep in his arms.

I must have moved about quite a lot in my sleep, for when I woke up about two hours later, my back was turned to Michel and the bedclothes had fallen off us. A cool evening breeze smelling of the countryside caressed our naked bodies.

'Are you asleep, darling?' he whispered.

'No, my love. I was wondering if you were awake,' I replied.

The young man's body was pressed close to mine, his belly against my buttocks, his mouth close to the nape of my neck. And it was obvious, quite obvious, that our recent skirmish had not diminished his ardour, quite the contrary! The serpent between Michel's thighs was fully awake and prodding my bare bottom with its blunt head.

'Darling, you're giving me an idea!' the young man whispered.

I laughed in a most unladylike way. There were a few ideas playing around in my mind too! The feel of that stiff organ prodding my behind was making me feel decidedly lewd. I wanted Michel to take me again.

But my lover's thoughts were not moving in the same direction as mine. Oh no! He had something much more perverse in mind! It soon became clear to me what he wanted to do when I felt him pressing my bottom-cheeks, separating them and gently opening them up so that he could inspect the mysterious region which they concealed.

'Michel, darling, what are you doing?' I said plaintively.

There was no need for him to reply: his fingers answered in his stead: they were busily engaged in exploring the dark crevice between my buttocks, and in particular, the orifice nestling there.

Then I gave a loud gasp of shock, for Michel had started to push his finger in where no man had ever previously been! He went on pushing, gently but firmly, until it was buried in me up to the hilt. Then he almost withdrew his finger, only to push it right back inside me again.

'Darling, please stop,' I pleaded. 'I don't like it!'

Which was certainly true! Michel was not really hurting me – he was being far too careful for that – but what he was doing seemed to me to be wrong.

However, my pleas did not deter him: he kept moving his finger in and out for some considerable time. Then the finger was withdrawn to be replaced by something much bigger, much more voluminous . . . His thumb? No, it was much too big for that! Was it possible? Surely Michel wouldn't go so far as to take me like that?

'Darling, please don't! Not that way!' I gasped, feeling a twinge of unease.

Not that I really felt inclined to put up any real resistance, but it was like losing one's virginity for the second time! Would my lover have any respect for me if I let him do that? That was what was really worrying me!

But it would have been impossible for me to resist Michel's desires for long. On the contrary, I now did my best to facilitate the operation, but that was not easy: there was a tremendous disproportion in size between the battering ram and the tiny orifice which it was trying to penetrate.

After a few more vain efforts, Michel lifted me up into a different position: I now knelt on all fours, my dishevelled hair spread upon the pillow. My uneasiness was beginning to give way to feelings of voluptuous pleasure.

Michel got into position on his knees behind me, then he lubricated the tip of his instrument, as well as my orifice, with some saliva. Then he tried again. This time his efforts were successful: suddenly I felt my rear passage being stretched, distended as the erect organ entered me.

'Oh, Michel, my love!' I gasped.

It was a most uncomfortable feeling, but the big thing relentlessly continued its progress, sliding in right to the very depths of my being and Michel too was gasping with the tightness of my gripping flesh.

I held on to the pillow for all I was worth, hoping that this endurance test would not last long.

He started to move in and out, back and forth, very, very slowly at first, then gradually increasing the pace until his stomach was beating a steady rhythm against my buttocks. Now something remarkable started to happen: the discomfort vanished, as if my well-stretched flesh had taken the measure of the invader. It was sliding back and forth much more easily now. Discomfort had become voluptuous pleasure, anxiety had been transformed into sweetness. My belly had become a hot sheath whose sole purpose was to accommodate the stiff serpent of flesh which was energetically plumbing its depths!

Michel slipped his hand between my thighs and began to caress my clitoris as he continued to thrust in and out. It was not long before I was palpitating in the throes of orgasm and, at that moment, the young man reached his peak, pouring himself into the depths of me!

When I recall this astonishing scene, which happened yesterday, I can't help wondering if my whole personality has changed. Farewell all conventional ideas! I have been possessed as never before and feel nothing but love for the man who possessed me!

Is Jacqueline Dambleuse becoming some sort of moral monster?

HE

What a strange day yesterday was! Jacqueline, who until then had been a sensual but *conventional* mistress, revealed an unexpected aspect of herself.

She banished all modesty or fear and abandoned herself to unbridled pleasure. She fell in docilely with whatever my voluptuous fancy dictated.

I have no idea what came over me: it must have been the stifling heat in that bedroom, as well as the effects of the food and wine we had consumed perhaps. At all events, the young woman became a shameless mistress, an ardent lover, willing to try anything!

We went up to the bedroom immediately we had finished our meal and I undressed my mistress straight away. Nothing could be more delightful than to see her magnificent body in its provocative nudity. I love those swelling breasts with their prominent nipples, that smooth belly, those full hips! She was showing herself to me completely naked, in broad daylight, for the first time. She exhibited herself to me without any attempt to conceal anything . . . the young woman seemed to be in a state of voluptuous intoxication.

Then she in her turn wanted to undress me. The feel of those delicate fingers busying themselves with my trouser buttons immediately aroused me. In next to no time I was naked and we got into bed.

I could see from Jacqueline's brightly shining eyes and wet, slack mouth that she was ready for anything. She proved it by immediately disappearing under the bedclothes in search of my virility, which she started to kiss warmly and enthusiastically.

I could feel her lips pressing themselves to my length as lightly as the wings of butterflies. Then suddenly she took the swollen tip into her mouth and started to suck it.

She had turned right round and her knees were pressing into the pillow on either side of my face. A sweet odour of amber mingled with warm flesh assailed my nostrils. Jacqueline's love-slit, with its covering of fair pubic hair, was but a few inches away from my face. The pale-pink, delicate lips attracted me like a mouth asking to be kissed.

Such an invitation could not be refused! I gripped her thighs and buried my face in the odorous love-nest.

Of course, making love in that position was nothing new to me. What was new was the perfect harmony which reigned between us. The rhythm of love took possession of us, carrying Jacqueline and me along in its flow. I opened the young woman's sex-lips with my fingers and kissed and tongued the pink orifice which was revealed to me. At the same time, Jacqueline was enthusaistically sucking my rigid weapon, her head bobbing up and down rhythmically.

Our mutual excitement was mounting to its peak. Jacqueline was moaning softly but continued to suck me as if her life depended upon it.

At last we could no longer contain ourselves, and as I unleashed myself into that wet, warm mouth, my own mouth was flooded with the young woman's love-juice, which added immeasurably to my own pleasure.

We were both sweating profusely. When Jacqueline emerged from under the bedclothes, her hair was dishevelled, her face flushed and she looked very pretty. What a strange little woman she is! Such an unusual combination of shyness and wantonness!

As she seemed tired, I took her in my arms, where she quickly fell asleep, a troubled sleep broken by groans and starts, which showed how agitated her whole being was.

At one stage, she rolled over suddenly, turning her back towards me. Those big soft bottom-cheeks pressing against my groin awoke a perverse desire within me. For a long time I lay there struggling against it, not wanting to risk upsetting Jacqueline by trying to do something which might shock her. But when the dear girl woke up, she seemed to be in such an aroused state that I hesitated no longer.

I slid my hand into the cleft between her buttocks. It seemed warm, moist and mysterious in there in that secret region. The organ which had been slumbering between my thighs twitched into life and was soon ready for action again.

Right in the depths of that valley of flesh, my exploring fingers soon encountered the secret orifice.

But when I tried to translate the caress into a bolder, more precise action, Jacqueline cried out in protest. It was quite obvious that no one had ever made love to her in such a fashion before.

Yet her protest somehow lacked conviction. An instinct told me that it would not take much persuasion to overcome the sweet girl's resistance. My instinct was right: a few kisses in the nape of her neck, a few whispered words of love soon overcame any objections.

Docilely, Jacqueline did as I asked and got into

position on all fours, head resting on the pillow, bottom sticking up and offered to me. What a charming sight that bottom was! But I sensed that she had mixed feelings concerning what we were about to do.

Several fruitless attempts resulted in some fresh protests on her part; however, she made no real effort to discourage me and held the position on all fours. My organ, far from being discouraged, was stiff to the point of bursting! At last, with the help of a plentiful lubrication of saliva, I managed to effect an entry.

Jacqueline's extreme tightness in that region was well calculated to stimulate as well as maintain my amorous rigidity. Nothing is more pleasing than to feel one's weapon gripped in a silky smooth ring of flesh, imprisoned in an exquisitely tight sheath!

My mistress gasped and moaned with mingled discomfort and sensual pleasure. I was buried right up to the hilt in the warm centre of those magnificent buttocks!

For a while, I just stayed quite still, enjoying the feel of that tightly gripping flesh. Then I started to move my organ in and out, but very slowly at first, taking the greatest care not to hurt her. It was only very gradually that I increased the speed of my movements.

As time went by, Jacqueling started to become more relaxed and the way in which she eventually began to move her hips in time with my thrusts showed that she was feeling sensual pleasure.

Never before had I experienced such intense voluptuousness! I soon reached my climax and over-flowed into Jacqueline's warm depths. She reached hers too, at the same moment. We lay side by side, panting and exhausted.

Do I despise the young woman for having so easily granted me this ultimate favour? If I did, I would be an imbecile because it was in fact the most wonderful thing she could have done for me.

Undoubtedly, sensuality as well as curiosity played their part in motivating her acquiescence but, nevertheless, I am certain that Jacqueline doesn't really like such unnatural love-making and that her real motive for giving in was to *please me*.

Ah, how grateful men should be to women on such occasions: when they do something they don't really enjoy, purely and simply to give us pleasure!

Don't be angry with me for what I did, Jacqueline darling. Men can be such dirty beasts sometimes. And women who understand that and indulge us give us the greatest proof of their love.

Epilogue

SHE

I feel both happy and unhappy at the same time. I have belonged to Michel and loved him for more than a fortnight now. Our love, which at first was so uncomplicated, soon sank into an ocean of forbidden pleasures. Perversion, cerebrality mingled with the simple sensuality of our encounters.

From the point of view of physical satisfaction, I can't complain. The perfect harmony which reigned between us from the start has only increased.

There's nothing we have not done, these hot summer nights. We have satisfied all our desires, every caprice, as if to do so were the most natural thing in the world.

I'm still intoxicated with kisses, exhausted with so much pleasure. Never have I felt so completely happy and satisfied!

Yet I am suffering at a deep level of my being, suffering because Michel doesn't really love me. I have suspected it all along, but now I'm certain. He enjoys himself with me; he enjoys himself a great deal. His senses are mine, but not his heart! Perhaps, soon, when we have run through the whole gamut of sensations, he will toss me aside like a plaything which has ceased to give pleasure.

Whose fault will that be? Mine possibly, for being too frank, too spontaneous, for giving myself too freely, for displaying my pleasure too openly.

Men are strange creatures! They like us to be responsive as well as beautiful. But if we show ourselves to be too experienced, too expert, they give us the cold shoulder – after having extracted every last ounce of pleasure from us, of course!

It seems to me that if you want a man to fall in love with you, you shouldn't start with sensuality.

As for me, I gave myself quite simply, without any preliminary reflexion. And, like so many women, I'm going to pay dearly for my indiscretion.

This evening, after makng love, we fell asleep in each other's arms. I did not sleep long, however. There were too many anxious thoughts buzzing around inside my head. When I woke up, I quietly switched on the bedside lamp and looked at my lover.

He was sleeping peacefully, like the child he had once been. Desires satisfied, completely relaxed, he had confidently abandoned himself to refreshing slumber.

For a long time, scarcely daring to breathe, I scrutinized that impassive face, the source of all my joy, and my suffering.

Then suddenly, without really knowing why, I was weeping. I wept silently, softly, with painful resignation. I wept to see Michel looking so peaceful, so mysterious. I wept because my love was too intense!

A river of tears rolled down my cheeks. Quiet sobs racked me. The tears were those of a woman who believed that her happiness was about to disappear.

★

HE

A deeply moving revelation! I awoke suddenly tonight, as if guided by some obscure prescience.

The bedside lamp was on. Jacqueline was looking at me, watching me sleep. I was immediately struck by the strange expression on her face, a face ravaged by profound misery. Great big tears were rolling down her cheeks, making the dear girl look even more movingly beautiful than usual.

'You're crying!' I said. 'Whatever's the matter, sweetheart? What's come over you?'

She tried to stem the flood of tears, but in vain. Embarrassed, completely overcome by her grief . . . and radiantly beautiful she said:

'I don't know, Michel . . . Watching you sleeping, I just started to cry . . . I think it's because I love you too much!'

What wonderful words! I think it must be the God of Love who has sent me those tears to enlighten me as to my true feelings!

'Jacqueline, my dearest love . . . My own baby, my only love!'

Overwhelmed with emotion, I took her in my arms and kissed her magnificent tears away.

At last I understood: I understood that I had been in love with Jacqueline all along, without realizing it. The high tide of our sensuality, our perfect physical harmony, had not given me time to crystallize my thoughts, my deepest feelings.

Those tears, offered by love, were for me an inestimable gift, and brought me the revelation. A woman who moans with voluptuous pleasure is only giving her body. But a woman who weeps is giving her entire being.

There is no more uncertainty in my mind now. Gone too are my scepticism and my cynicism.

We are looking forward to a marvellous future together, for our perfect physical entente has been immeasurably heightened, intensified by the radiant certainty of our love.

Nocturnal Pleasures

Foreword

Comfortably installed in their leather armchairs, three men were smoking and chatting.

The cosy atmosphere in the little room with its haze of tobacco smoke, the soft light of the lamp, the glittering night sky, which could be seen through the open window, was conducive to the sharing of secrets.

Gustave Chauvelard, the industrialist's son, was there, a worthy representative of the solid French bourgeoisie: clean-shaven, pink-cheeked, already pot-bellied in his well-cut dinner-jacket, with his pipe clenched between his teeth and wearing horn-rimmed spectacles, he seemed like a debonair bulldog.

Gontran, Marquis de Longuelade, was there too. Tall, slim, elegant, hair growing thin, a monocle jammed into his left eye, he personified marvellously the ancient nobility which had been forced to come to terms with the twentieth century.

And, finally, there was Jacques Duvernier. Looking impeccable in his evening-suit, with well-groomed hair which was silver at the temples, pleasing, regular features, he had the perfect physique of the ladies' man. His fine, caressing eyes revealed an enthusiasm for living, while a sensual mouth indicated an enthusiasm for savouring life. The suggestion of inner torment which one could sometimes read in the expression on his face, in no way decreased this handsome man's attractiveness.

Naturally, they were talking about women. Chauvelard and Longuelade had a lot to say because they didn't know much about them.

Duvernier listened because he knew a great deal about the fair sex.

'In short,' said the Marquis, with a certain complacency, 'women hold no more surprises for me. Once they've taken their clothes off and got into bed, they're all the same: all they want is to have a good come!'

Duvernier shook his head and said, in a condescending tone:

'Don't you believe it, my dear fellow! My experience is quite the opposite: every naked woman, moaning with pleasure, reveals something different about herself and her country of origin.'

Chauvelard laughed.

'To listen to you, one would think you'd done a tour of the world of cunt!'

Duvernier ignored his friend's coarseness.

'I have known women in many different countries,' he said gravely. 'Before setting out on my travels, I resolved to spend four nights with whatever lovely foreigners might chance to cross my path. In that way, it would be possible for me to really get to know them, and establish comparisons. I had some very strange experiences.'

'Oh, do tell!' said Chauvelard. 'I'm all ears!'

'Yes, go on,' said Gontran de Longuelade. 'I'd love to hear what happened!'

Jaques Duvernier smiled slyly.

'I'm not in the habit of divulging my bedroom secrets or boasting about my amorous conquests,' he

90

said. 'However, since you've asked me, and we've nothing better to do, I don't mind telling you about some of my experiences, but you must not be shocked by my frankness.

'You will see that no two women are the same, and if their sighs of ecstacy resemble each other, their ways of attaining that ecstacy differ considerably.'

'Come on then, Don Juan, tell us all about it,' said Chauvelard. 'We're waiting!'

'We're all ears, my dear chap,' said Gontran de Longuelade.

So, while the stars shone in the night sky outside, Jacques Duvernier began his story.

English Pleasures

I shall begin, with your permission, by telling you about something which happened in England. The story doesn't really have an ending, so let's hope it doesn't disappoint you.

I was spending a few days with some friends who possessed a seaside villa at Folkestone. It is not my intention to bore you with a detailed account of my holiday. This typically English family included an ugly, sport-loving daughter, as well as two tall lads with rosy cheeks and sentimental souls. Porridge was served for breakfast every morning, the vicar came to lunch every Sunday and the Prince of Wales was always spoken of with the greatest respect: that's English families for you!

From the very first day, I was a bit worried about how to fill up the long hours, for there seemed to be very few distractions. Then they took me to the tennis club, which reassured me somewhat. Young people from the best families in the locality met at this club towards the end of every afternoon. Among them was a respectable number of young women who, it must be admitted, were far from resembling my hosts' sporty daughter.

In England there are no middle-of-the-road women: they're either frightful or ravishingly beautiful!

Certain young ladies at the tennis club fell into the latter category. There was one who especially appealed to me.

Try to imagine a woman bearing a close resemblance to those ladies who Helleu used to paint: tall, slender and supple, she had very fine features, as well as that 'peaches and cream' complexion which is only to be found in her country. She was only nineteen and possessed big blue innocent eyes; her lips were rather thin, but well-shaped.

Under the thin material of the summer dress, big breasts quivered as she walked. It was easy for me to imagine how white, how soft to the touch they must be! Her buttocks were very feminine too and swayed seductively as she walked.

That lovely creature immediately became the object of all my hopes.

Fortunately, she did not find me displeasing. We played three sets and she won all of them, which undoubtedly made me appear sympathetic to her.

Who cared about winning a few games of tennis when something much more important was at stake!

After the tennis, we all piled into a couple of cars and drove to the beach. I made sure that I was sitting next to my recent adversary. Little was known to me about her except that her name was Jessie and that she played an excellent backhander.

Immediately, like the good Frenchman I am, I began paying her compliments. She listened to me indifferently, manifesting neither pleasure nor displeasure. Irritated by such apathy, I proposed a rendezvous for that evening.

She looked at me coldly.

'You're off your head!' she said drily.

Feeling somewhat embarrassed, I shut up and

didn't breathe a word until we arrived at the beach. But later, when it was time to go home, my English miss approached me and, without betraying the least sign of emotion, said:

'Do you sometimes come for a walk here in the evening?'

'Yes,' I replied eagerly.

'So do I . . . sometimes,' she said.

And that was all. But that evening, after having given the slip to my two Cadum Babies and their sporty sister, I went for a stroll along the beach and who should I see walking nonchalantly towards me but Jessie!

'Oh, fancy seeing you here!' she exclaimed, without the slightest trace of irony.

'Yes, indeed,' I replied politely.

I was beginning to get into the English way of doing things!

Side by side, we began to walk along the sandy beach together. She walked with long, graceful strides, like a thoroughbred horse. From time to time, her arm brushed against mine.

Night had fallen; stars glittered in the sky above the sea, which was as calm as a lake.

Jessie looked at me appraisingly.

'You walk almost as well as an Englishman,' she remarked.

After about a quarter of an hour of walking and far from brilliant conversation, I suggested that we should have a rest.

'If you like,' said the young woman, in a tone of complete indifference.

It so happened that there was a nice little spot between two sand dunes where we would be both comfortable and concealed from inquisitive eyes. We went over to it and sat down.

To be honest, the girl's unrelenting coldness might have paralysed my audacity if it had not been for the fact that I recalled an old adage which says that anything goes with English girls so long as one talks to them about something else at the same time.

So I skilfully turned the conversation to the subject of tennis and spent five minutes congratulating Jessie upon her style. We also discussed technique in general.

She seemed very interested and while we were speaking, my hands wandered.

I started by stroking the young lady's thighs, whose warmth I could feel through the thin summer dress.

'It's quite obvious that you've got a special gift for playing tennis,' I said, suddenly putting my arm round her waist.

She didn't appear to notice it, and launched into an enthusaistic account of the history of the game in England.

As she was speaking, I started to caress her breasts with my left hand . . . Very nice breasts they were too, big and firm. The nipples were extremely prominent; I held one of them between my finger and thumb, which was easy to do through the thin material of the dress. I squeezed it gently, that delightful raspberry!

Jessie's lips tightened and, for a moment, her whole body contracted. Then she went on speaking about tennis. I understood then that I was following the correct procedure.

'We've got some good players in France,' I said: 'Borotra, Bousous, Merlin . . .'

Meanwhile, my hand had abandoned the young

woman's breasts and was now resting on her knee, close to the hem of the skirt.

Then, while praising Borotra's game, I insinuated my hand under Jessie's dress.

How delightful it was to feel those bare thighs, which were warm and smooth as satin. Voluptuous feelings filled me; my virility rose to the occasion!

I continued to move upward under the skirt. Suddenly, my fingers encountered the lacy border of a pair of knickers.

Pushing audacity even further, I slipped my hand under the pretty girl's buttocks. Jessie had helped me by almost mechanically raising her bottom.

Naturally, I continued to perorate, but it was not easy to concentrate, for the last thing which concerned me at that moment was the game of tennis and its champions.

The English girl was now sitting on my hand and I savoured the feel of those magnificent buttocks in their covering of thin silk.

But it was my intention to go much further. With the greatest care, I manoeuvered my fingers so that they were resting on her mound: I could feel the bush of pubic hair underneath the knickers.

In spite of Jessie's apparent impassivity, she quivered. Yet I hesitated to put my hand inside her knickers. Something in her manner made me feel that that would be going too far.

In fact, the young woman's unbending attitude was beginning to irritate me; however, I was not going to give up without making a further effort. Using two fingers, I started to caress the English girl's sex through the protective covering of silk, without breaking off the conversation however.

She began to show signs of responding to that intimate caress.

Then suddenly she closed her thighs, imprisoning my hand between them.

'Yes,' the young woman was saying, 'there is no doubt that Perry is a very good player . . . but I think you're going too far!'

Feeling rather intimidated, I made as if to withdraw my hand.

'No . . . it's all right,' said Jessie, but without any warmth.

Her unpredictable behaviour rather amused me. I squeezed closer to the English miss and with my free hand titillated her nipples, which were now quite hard, while my other hand moved around freely inside her knickers.

By this time, we had run out of conversation. Jessie was lying on her back looking up at the starry sky. She was breathing precipitately, breasts rising and falling, lips parted.

Suddenly, she closed her eyes and gave a plaintive sigh. Once again the young woman's thighs closed on my hand, while she shuddered in the throes of an orgasm.

I was filled with an exultant sense of victory at having overcome the English girl's prudishness. I wanted to kiss her, to put my tongue in her mouth, but Jessie's strong hands pushed me away.

'Don't be disgusting!' she snapped. 'You're not my fiancé! You can't kiss me!'

I nearly burst out laughing at this curious display of puritan hypocrisy. There was no doubt about it, Jessie was certainly English!

We walked back slowly, without saying much to each other. My desire had not been satisifed, but I had a distinct feeling that it would be better to let things rest as they were that evening.

We met again the next evening and by a tacit accord, went back to the same spot.

The moonlight was beautiful: one could see everything as plainly as if it were the middle of the day. That made it possible to see just how ravishingly lovely Jessie was. She wore a light dress of white muslin and a silk ribbon kept her hair in place.

She sat down first and looked up at me with a smile.

'Tell me some more about tennis in France,' she said.

I didn't have to be asked twice! I sat down and took her in my arms. It was immediately obvious that Jessie had abandoned some of her reserve, for she did not attempt any resistance. In spite of what had happened the previous night, I tried to kiss her on the mouth; she tried to prevent me from doing so, but without much conviction. Finally, she gave in and offered me her lips.

Our mouths were joined in a passionate kiss. The lovely girl's breath was sweet and it was not long before we were exploring each other's mouth with our tongues.

For a long time we continued this delightful pastime. It seemed to last forever. Meanwhile, I had put my hand boldly up Jessie's skirt. What a lovely surprise! My prudish little English miss wasn't wearing any knickers!

She opened her thighs, offering her unprotected love-nest to me. My probing fingers encountered a forest of short, springy pubic hair. Then I started to stroke the sex-lips, which were already moist and half open.

Jessie kissed me even more passionately, while her arms tightened about me.

Gradually, I had started to masturbate the young woman, using my fingers to rub her increasingly wet sex, then titillating her clitoris.

She wriggled excitedly, breathing in short gasps. At last, she had a violent orgasm, drenching my fingers with love-dew, gripping me tightly, gasping and moaning with joy.

After a while, she disengaged herself and looked at me coldly.

'You're not a gentleman,' was all she said.

That evening, I was not permitted to take any more liberties.

The next night, I arrived at the beach with a plan of campaign already worked out in my head. The young woman's attitude of passive acceptance, while giving me nothing in return, was really getting me down! I had resolved to bring matters to a head, even if it meant risking a quarrel with the egotistical young miss.

As soon as we arrived at our favourite spot, I set about making love to Jessie in earnest, kissing her passionately, using my tongue with considerable expertise. I kissed her mouth, her cheeks, her eyes, her ears, her forehead. Meanwhile, my hands were busy fondling those lovely breasts as well as the shapely bottom.

It was not long before Jessie began to respond to such ardent love-making. Her gasping breath and ecstatic cries made me realize that the propitious moment had arrived. It was now or never!

As unobtrusively as possible, I undid my fly buttons and liberated my magic wand.

Jessie was unaware of what was happening. Then

when I took her hand in mind and gently guided it to my provocative nudity, she gave a scream of horror!

She screamed, but did not run away. The young lady was far too excited for that! Suddenly, her fingers grasped 'the thing.' That contact overwhelmed Jessie, banishing all thoughts of modesty from her mind. Breathing hard, she began to caress me, very clumsily but with a lot of goodwill.

Meanwhile, I had slipped my hand under her skirt and was returning the courtesy.

Then the English girl became even more excited. She couldn't seem to get over having discovered the male organ of generation. She was handling it with increasing confidence and dexterity; sometimes roughly, sometimes caressing, her hands awoke a strange voluptuousness in me.

A voluptuousness Jessie shared, judging by that young lady's cries and contortions as I came.

A few minutes passed, broken only by the sound of our breathing. Suddenly, Jessie stood up, smoothing her crumpled skirt.

'You're a terrible pig!' she said, in a voice shaking with anger.

Then she ran off so fast that it was impossible for me to catch up with her.

Yet, the next night, this strange girl was on the jetty. But I noticed that she was now wearing a charming jacket and slacks: the latter were very form-hugging, very revealing, but they would effectively prevent any access to the young lady's secret charms.

'Come along,' she said. 'I want to talk to you.'

She dragged me off into the darkness . . . but this time we didn't go to our usual place.

She stopped half way along the beach, turned to me and said:

'Are you going to marry me, Jacques?'

This question rather surprised me. I had, in fact, decided long since to remain a bachelor all my life, but couldn't bring myself to say so point-blank.

'Well, you know . . . marriage,' I stammered.

'Very well,' she said icily. 'Goodbye!'

I automatically grasped the hand she extended to me. But as she turned her back on me and was walking away, I hastened after the young woman.

'Listen, Jessie,' I said, 'you must try to understand . . .'

She turned to face me and nailed me to the spot with her steely blue eyes.

'If you don't leave me alone, I'll call a policeman!' she hissed venomously.

Discouraged beyond words by such an attitude, I had no alternative but to let her go. Thus ended my fourth night of love!

You must find this story very flat, since its ending is not what you were expecting. I have told it to you, however, because I think it is an admirable illustration of what the character of the average English girl is like: caress her as audaciously as you like; she won't mind if you keep talking about something else, for then, to her way of thinking, appearances have been saved; kissing the young lady may prove to be a little more difficult since, for English females, the kiss is a veritable communion of souls; if you try to go farther, she'll drag you in front of a minister! And should you refuse, she'll cut you stone dead the next time you meet.

Spanish Pleasures

A few days later, I was in Spain. This hot and colourful land offers a kaleidoscope of picturesque specatacles to the traveller. It was not my first visit, but I had not had any amorous adventures before.

I was staying at a small spa town in the mountains for a few days. The surrounding landscape was not harsh, neither was it lacking in grandeur. The streets of the little town were rustic and tortuous; everything was bathed in warm, golden sunlight. The women were pretty, it was good to be alive!

The hotel where I was staying was very picturesque, not especially clean, but the dirt formed part of the charm. The food was heavily seasoned with spices which aroused the senses, while the oppressively hot nights exacerbated unsatisfied desires.

The maid on my floor, a truly magnificent girl, presented all the characteristics of the race: her bronzed skin recalled that of a gypsy. Her hair, which was held back by a headband, was jet-black, as were her provocatively, laughing eyes. The young woman's mouth was large, well-shaped and extremely sensual.

She wore a flowered blouse which revealed more than it concealed two lovely firm breasts with aggressively pointing nipples. What her legs were like it was impossible to say, for they were concealed by a long skirt as well as multiple petticoats, such as all the local girls wore. But I sometimes caught a glimpse of slender ankles, one of which was encircled by a fine golden chain.

Someone told me that she was seventeen, but she could easily have passed for twenty-one.

The day I arrived, a fiesta was in full swing in the little town. In the market square I saw the girl dancing with some other local girls. She had made herself especially pretty for the occasion. Excessively made-up, she looked like some exotic flower in the bright sunshine.

The lovely young woman danced proudly to the accompaniment of some guitars, her little red high-heeled shoes beating a tattoo on the ground, hips swaying rhythmically.

When she whirled round, the long skirt and petti-coats lifted up, giving one a tantalizing glimpse of long, shapely brown legs.

That was enough to arouse my desire and I made up my mind there and then to become the young woman's lover as soon as possible.

The same evening, having retired early, I rang for the maid, intending to ask for a jug of hot water. She appeared, looking very happy after her day at the fiesta.

I made up my mind not to beat about the bush. I stood up and went over to her and saw that there was no sign of fear in the young woman's eyes. When I caught hold of her wrists, she made no effort to withdraw them. On the contrary she drew close to me, setting my senses on fire!

An odour of musk, mingled with perspiration arose from her body, which intoxicated me even further.

I leaned forward and kissed her on the mouth. The full lips were delightfully moist and incredibly soft.

The girl responded ardently, without any hesitation. Her tongue filled my mouth, like a warm, palpitating little animal. That tongue explored every corner of my mouth with a quite incredible skill. We were now locked in a close embrace and she could undoubtedly feel my rigid organ pressing against her stomach, but she made no attempt to pull away.

I felt pretty certain that this was a quite experienced young woman. Gradually, still embracing and kissing her, I manoeuvered her towards the bed, then we sank down together upon it.

She was giggling excitedly. In no time at all, I had worked the long skirt up to her waist, revealing a pair of smooth brown thighs, which were a delight to look at!

She was wearing a pair of very brief, pink silk knickers, decorated with ribbons and lace. Then my companion rolled over, still giggling, presenting me with a lovely view of two magnificent buttocks tightly encased in silk!

How that excited me! I pulled her close and started kissing her again.

As we kissed, she quivered with voluptuous pleasure and murmured some words in Spanish, which I didn't understand. Our bellies were pressed close together, her legs were entwined with mine.

That girl of the people was exciting me more than the most refined mistress could have done. Perhaps it was because she seemed to me to be so typically Spanish: hot, strong, of unlimited sensuality, full of perfumes and passion . . .

After a while, I stopped kissing the girl's full lips, turning my attention to her palpitating bosom. I undid some buttons and had soon uncovered one of her breasts: it was round and soft and crowned with a dark pointing nipple. I began to kiss it, then to suck it.

The girl arched her back; she was panting as I continued to suck the ripe fruit.

At length, I abandoned the breast and turned my attention to those lovely brown thighs. I knelt beside the bed, covering them with passionate kisses. My lips brushed the lace of her knickers, then I buried my face in her crotch and began to suck her sex through its silken covering. My hands were not idle either: they were busily engaged in fondling the girl's bottom which was wriggling with pleasure.

It seemed to me that nothing could go wrong then. But when I attempted to consumate our passion a few moments later, I met with serious disappointment. The lovely Spanish girl slipped out of my arms, leapt off the bed and pulled her skirt down.

'You must excuse me, senor!' she said.

'Someone is ringing for me.'

Then she was gone.

I sat up, waiting for her return. I rang the bell several times, but she didn't reappear. My desire was not to be satisfied that night.

'In short, it was a case of *Woman and Puppet!*' said Chauvelard mockingly.

Duvernier smiled.

'Perhaps,' he said. 'Then again, perhaps not.'

The famous novel by Pierre Louys came to my mind too that night. Funnily enough, the maid's name was Concha, just like the heroine in the book! I was curious to see what would happen next.

The next night, as you may guess, I didn't fail to

ring for my Concha . . . Not that she really was mine, yet!

She seemed to have forgotten what had happened the previous evening and gave me a charming smile.

I indicated that she should close the door and come to me, which the young woman did without hesitation.

As on the previous evening, I kissed her, at the same time manoeuvering her towards the bed.

For the next few minutes, our kisses and embraces were too much of a repetition of those of the previous evening for me to inflict a description of them upon you. Suffice it to say that we arrived at the same point as before: the girl moaning and writhing beside me, my virility stiff with desire . . .

I was curious to know whether it was through fear or calculation that she had refused to yield to me the previous night. I made a determined effort to pull her pretty little knickers down.

Unfortunately, the young woman was equally determined that they were staying where they were and a brief struggle ensued, which resulted in a victory for me since I was stronger. It was a hollow victory, however: I have always detested violence and would get no pleasure in taking what a woman is not prepared to give of her own free will.

She looked up at me with tears sparkling in her lovely dark eyes.

'You are no gentleman!' she said angrily.

'And you're no lady to lead me on so!' I retorted equally angrily. 'You'd better put these back on,' I said, thrusting the knickers into her hand.

She made no move to do so, but continued to lie there looking up at me.

'I had no intention of leading you on,' she said quietly. 'But you must realize, señor, that in a village

106

like this a girl's life would be unbearable, unliveable, if she became a mother without being married!'

Comprehension dawned on me. I smiled at the young woman reassuringly.

'You don't need to worry about getting pregnant with me, Concha,' I said. 'Haven't you ever heard of "coitus interruptus?" '

'No senor,' she replied. 'What is it?'

'It means, my child,' said I, 'that when a man is about to come, he pulls his staff out of the girl's love-nest then sprinkles his seed on her belly. That's what I would do if you let me make love to you.'

Concha looked dubious.

'How could I be sure that you really would pull out?' she said.

Hope was reborn within me, for what Concha was saying indicated that she was at least open to argument.

From a long experience of this kind of situation, I knew that patience combined with skilful caresses was the best approach, so I lay down beside the young woman, took her in my arms, and continued the argument to the accompaniment of kisses and caresses. As we talked, my fingers stroked those lovely smooth thighs, then moved even higher where they encountered the lips of that other more secret mouth.

Gradually, Concha lost interest in the argument; her words turned into sighs. My fingers were wet with her juices.

I realized then that she was ready to give me what I wanted. I quickly slipped my trousers off and got between her open thighs. Cool fingers guided me to the right place, then I was buried in warm silken flesh, right up to the hilt!

She was certainly no virgin, but her love-sheath

gripped my virility quite tightly. Concha did not just lie there passively; she moved responsively, sighing and moaning. Her body clung to mine; we were moist with perspiration. I have never made love to a more passionate woman! Her plump bottom moved in time with my thrusts; her hands clasped my back, or buried themselves in my hair. She was gasping and crying out more and more loudly.

I was getting pretty close to the moment when it would be so easy to shoot my seed into that palpitating love-sheath, but it was not my intention to break the promise I had freely given to Concha. Love should give people pleasure, not ruin their lives!

The young woman was now so excited that it would indeed have been easy for me to come inside her; so I must take care not to lose control.

When the orgasm hit her, I thought she was going to pass out! What a furty of passionate writhing flesh! Her sex was so hot and overflowing! I held on as long as possible, in order not to spoil her pleasure, then I had to pull out of it would have been too late.

In fact, it was not a moment too soon! My rigid sex spurted and spurted: it seemed as though it would never stop. Long jets of virile liquid landed on Concha's breasts and belly.

At last, however, it was over. Our desires had been satisfied, for a while anyway, and we lay there on the bed for quite some time, resting after our exertions. She could not stay with me all night, of course, but you may be sure I slept well after her departure.

Concha came back the next night, and the night after that. Each time we made love in the same way, with me practising coitus interruptus, for which the young woman was very grateful. She taught me nothing new, nothing perverse. We just made love in a straightforward, uncomplicated way.

The fifth day after my arrival at the little town, I said goodbye to Concha and set off on my travels again. Making love to the fiery Spanish girl had been a delightful experience, but I was badly in need of rest and recuperation!

Egyptian Pleasures

I can still see the scene, as if it had only taken place yesterday. Yet five years have passed already. But a memory of sensual sweetness lingers in my mind and I think I can smell the heavy perfumes of the East mingling with the odour of hot sand and Love.

Cairo . . . I had arrived the previous day and installed myself in a palatial hotel. My plan of campaign was divided into two parts: one of them, inspired by purely aesthetic considerations, consisted of admiring the thousands of artistic marvels of the country; the other, much more down-to-earth, consisted of seeking to satisfy my desire for pretty women and finding love in the hot Egyptian sunshine.

I had already seen a goodly number of admirable women at the hotel: not many of them were French – alas, our country is poor! – but there were a lot of Americans and Englishwomen, as well as a few Scandinavians. Almost all of these ladies were young, pretty, elegant.

The day after my arrival, I was to take part in an excursion to see the Sphinx and the Pyramids, which we were to contemplate, as was customary, in the rays of the setting sun, then under the starry night sky.

It must be admitted that aesthetic considerations were not my sole motive for going on the excursion:

I had read somewhere, and various friends had confirmed it, that the proximity of the Pyramids can have a very *particular* effect on women, and that some surprising mysteries were unveiled in the shadow of the great Sphinx!

Anyway, I was not alone: there were four of us and, by an almost unheard-of stoke of good luck, I was the only man, the three other travellers being ladies.

Naturally, two guides accompanied us: two solidly-built young chaps, upon whom the burnous conferred a certain majesty, contradicted by their vivacious, laughing eyes, which gleamed in their brown faces.

One of them introduced me to my fellow travellers, and I could hardly conceal my joy as I shook hands with them.

It would be difficult to say which was the most beautiful, because they were all splendid.

The first was a fabulously rich American divorcee: her name was Ethel Wasforth. She was tall, very distinguished-looking, with lovely chestnut hair, brown eyes, a firm chin and a small but exquisitely well-shaped mouth. She wore a long white travelling coat, made of very light cloth, and a sun-helmet was perched on her head.

The name of the second lady was Astrid Rasmussen, undoubtedly Swedish; she had hair like golden corn and her eyes were the same limpid blue as the sky. She was not wearing a dress but was clad in riding-breeches, which were made of white buckskin, very tight, that revealed her plump buttocks. An extremely thin silk blouse did little to conceal an admirable bosom. Highly polished leather boots and a white hat completed this amazonian outfit.

The third lady was the one who most attracted me. She could not have been older than twenty. She too

111

was an American and a marvellous example of the modern liberated young woman whose bank account is overflowing with dollars and whose daddy is a planter somewhere in Florida. This young lady wasn't very tall but admirably well-formed. She had pretty features and a knowing look in her eyes. Her name was May Clarence.

I couldn't take my eyes off her: she looked very attractive in a light white two-piece dress.

As regards the first part of our excursion, there is little to tell. We were taken to our destination in a small charabanc. The three ladies sat and chatted together, while I sat with the guides.

We broke our journey at the Home Restaurant, which was there for the benefit of tourists. We partook of a cold repast accompanied by an excellent champagne, to which we did full justice. Mrs Wasforth bought ten bottles, which she said would fortify us during the rest of the journey. That seemed promising!

When we left the restaurant, some camels were waiting for us.

Little did those creatures of the desert realize what precious burdens they were to carry that evening!

Our little caravan set off at a very middling pace. I brought up the rear with our two guides, which gave me a good opportunity to look at the three women in front of me. Swaying on their camels as if they were sailing, they clung to the pommels of their saddles, laughing excitedly.

They all sat astride. For Astrid, in her riding-breeches, that was quite natural, although it made her plump bottom look even more enticing.

But as far as the other ladies were concerned, sitting astride like that proved to be very revealing! Ethel

Wasforth's travelling-coat was pulled half way up her thighs. However closely I looked, I could see no trace of lingerie, or even a dress! Could she be naked underneath that lightweight coat?

As for May Clarence, her skirt had risen very high, but she made not the slightest attempt to pull it back down! After having regaled myself with the spectacle of the American girl's skirt stretched tightly over her charming buttocks, I urged my camel on and came up level with her. While we conversed about various things of little importance, I stared boldly at the secrets revealed by that raised skirt: pretty pink suspenders held May's stockings up. Above the gossamer tissue, two plump white thighs were visible, as well as a pair of dear little white silk knickers trimmed with lace.

My virility stood up in deference to those charms, and I found myself envying the camel for having such an intimate contact with the girl.

Travelling like that upon 'a ship of the desert,' seemed to have put May Clarence into a joyful mood. Everything amused her and she laughed loudly.

Astrid seemed very happy too . . . As for the lovely Mrs Wasforth, I thought she was a bit on edge. Her bare legs gripped the animal convulsively and with every shake and jerk, a strangely voluptuous expression came to the young woman's face. Was this bumpy journey giving her sensual pleasure?

At length, we arrived at our destination. The Pyramids rose up majestically before us against the blue of the sky. Their age-old stone was the same colour as the hot sand which surrounded us like an ocean. Impressed by so much beauty, we contemplated the grandiose monuments with their simple lines, beside which the Sphinx is eternally on guard.

For a while, my lovely companions and I forgot all about love.

The guides unloaded the camels, set up the tents in the sand and prepared the encampment for the night.

While Astrid and Ethel were repairing their make-up, I flirted a bit with May. But the American girl was something of an enigma to me: I already knew that Yankee girls were very free in their words and attitudes, but what lay behind that facade?

Then the guides called us to admire the setting sun. It was a truly wonderful sight: the great ball of fire sank slowly below the horizon. The desert was bathed in its orange rays. The Pyramids and the Sphinx, caressed by those rays, seemed for a few moments to be radiant with a supernatural light. Gradually, however, the fiery light diminished, then disappeared altogether.

It seemed to me that May Clarence had been particularly impressed by the spectacle, and I saw a tremor run through her body.

Our dinner was a happy affair. We did full justice to the excellent food. We also drank copiously of the American lady's champagne.

I don't know whether it was the effect of that heady wine, or the majesty of the hot night which covered us like a dark veil, but we were very tense, over-excited, as if a kind of amorous anguish was electrifying our senses.

Constellations of stars glittered brightly in the sky. A blessed torpor affected everything, both animate and inanimate. Quite close to where we were the imposing mass of the Pyramids rose up against the starry sky.

An Egyptian night . . . Astrid Rasmussen got up

first. She breathed deeply, stretching like a cat in the heavy darkness. Then she walked away, unaccompanied, in the direction of the Sphinx.

One of the guides smiled and winked suggestively at his colleague. Then he got to his feet in a leisurely fashion and strolled away whistling in the same direction.

A few moments later, I too walked over to the Sphinx, urged on by irresistible curiosity.

I approached the enigmatic monument slowly and sauntered along one side of it. I could hear someone whispering quite close to me. So I advanced cautiously to the corner stone and, taking good care not to be seen, looked round it.

There, very close in the darkness, it was just possible to make out two white forms. Then, at that precise moment, my friend, the moon, shone down upon them, revealing clearly just what was happening.

The pretty Swedish girl was locked in the guide's arms, her mouth pressed to his in a long, passionate kiss. At length, she pulled away, breathing heavily, and started to unfasten her belt. I saw the riding-breeches slide down those fine hips, to form a heap round her ankles. Astrid's body looked almost incredibly white in the moonlight. I savoured the spectacle of that lovely body: the firm buttocks, the curving belly and, between the thighs, an imprecise triangle of pubic hair.

For a moment, she rested her naked buttocks against the stone. The guide had shed his burnous. He approached the girl, then merged with her in a passionate embrace.

They were now coupled, standing up at the foot of the great Sphinx. I watched the undulations of their naked bodies, and listened to gasps and moans of the Swedish girl in the warm night air.

The spectacle excited me so much that I could no longer bear to watch it; moreover, I felt somewhat ashamed at playing the voyeur.

I walked back slowly towards the tents. But as I drew near to them, another passionate threnody reached my ears.

Ethel Wasforth was lying on her back without any modesty, completely naked! The young woman's travelling-coat was spread out on the sand beneath her and she was responding passionately to the other guide's love-making.

The man was completely naked too. What an unforgettable sight, those two bodies locked together, moving rhythmically in the throes of love in the Egyptian night!

The American woman was crying aloud now, crying out in pleasure, quite unconcerned about the possibility of anyone hearing! Her buttocks were responding enthusiastically to the guide's energetic thrusts.

So where was May? Guided by an intuitive feeling, I approached the other tent. The girl was there, lying flat on her stomach in the sand, peering round the canvas and watching the young couple's frolics with avid curiousity.

She was unaware of my presence. Suddenly, unable to bear it any longer, she rolled over on her side, without losing sight of the exciting spectacle. Feverishly, the girl pulled up her skirt then took her knickers off. Uttering small, childlike cries and using agile fingers, she strove to obtain sensual satisfaction.

Now was the moment to intervene! I lay down as

unobtrusively as possible on the sand, then placed my hand on May's bare arm.

The girl uttered a soft cry and swung round to face me. For a few seconds, she looked at me in astonishment. Then suddenly, with a sigh of happiness, she came into my arms, pressing herself right up against my body.

We kissed long and passionately. May's lips were as fresh as the sea, as soft as those of that other mouth concealed between her thighs. We used our tongues and the American girl proved that she was no novice in the art of kissing.

When I made as if to go further, my partner suddenly became nervous and unwilling. A scruple assailed me: perhaps May Clarence was a virgin! If that was the case, I had no desire to take advantage of her, for deflowering rich Yankee virgins can be a dangerous pastime, if one is not keen on the idea of getting married!

So I decided to sacrifice my own pleasure. I gently undid the girl's blouse, exposing two small but well-rounded breasts which looked very pale in the moonlight. I sucked each nipple in turn, feeling them swell and harden in my mouth.

May quivered, her soft voice moaned with pleasure. Slowly but surely, I moved downwards, kissing all the while . . .

At length, my mouth encountered the light down of pubic hair at the base of the stomach. I rained sweet kisses upon it and my partner became more and more excited. Then I took possession of the secret treasure.

May was sobbing with joy. The rosy petals of her sex opened to my exploring lips like a flower to sunlight. It seemed to me to have a taste of springtime. For a long time, I explored that intimate region with my tongue until the young woman went rigid then came, with a long wailing cry of release.

Afterwards, she lay there, eyes closed, exhausted. I disengaged myself, then very paternally pulled her skirt back down, found a blanket and tucked her up for the night.

What was I going to do now? My unselfish behaviour had done nothing to satisfy my desire.

Oh well, perhaps the best thing would be to try and get some sleep.

I moved away from the American girl so as not to be tempted and went and lay down in the sand some distance away. I lay on my back looking up at the bright starry sky. The throbbing rigidity between my thighs refused to subside.

But suddenly, I became aware of a naked womanly form approaching me. Was I dreaming? Then a warm body lay down beside me, pressing itself against my body. It was Ethel Wasforth, the insatiable Ethel, who had come to see what making love with a Frenchman would be like.

To be honest, although she was desirable, very desirable, the idea of having her when she had just been possessed by another man did not much appeal to me.

But the lovely American woman must have guessed what I was thinking, for she turned her back towards me, then started to undulate her big soft bottom against my rigid staff.

I pulled away a bit in order to contemplate that lovely curving white back, the slender waist, the swelling buttocks, separated by a dark, mysterious valley.

It was impossible to resist such invitingly offered

charms. My hands started to caress those magnificent buttocks.

Then I grasped them and gently but firmly eased them apart, so that I could slide my virility into the narrow passage.

The lovely Ethel must have been a devotee of such perverse games, because my organ slid in quite easily and she was already well-lubricated there. She was soon crying out ecstactically as I started to move in and out. The young woman moved her rump lasciviously in time with my thrusts.

It was not long before the supreme pleasure overtook me; my desire, too long contained, spurted out into that wet, warm, wriggling orifice.

Ethel reached her climax at the same moment, for the young woman's fingers were rubbing her clitoris.

When it was all over, we lay there in the sand for quite some time, exhausted by so much pleasure. Minutes passed, hours, perhaps, yet still we did not move. The moon hid its face behind a small cloud, shocked no doubt by our grossly indecent behaviour.

Duvernier was silent. His friends had been following his story with passionate interest, without once interrupting.

'And the next day?' said Gontran, adjusting his monocle. 'Which of the ladies, er . . .?'

Duvernier smiled.

'It was May Clarence,' he said. 'When we were back in Cairo, the next night, she turned up in my room at the hotel without batting an eyelid. With disarming frankness, she informed me that she was not a virgin and offered to prove it!

'For three whole nights, the young lady was my mistress – an exquisitely refined and responsive mistress.

'Nevertheless, nice as they were, those three nights of love did not make me forget our first contact: those delightful moments when I drank her femininity, crouching on the sand, watched by the indifferent eyes of the Sphinx.'

American Pleasures

We had just arrived in our tenth night-club that evening.

Already, some of the most celebrated establishments on Broadway had been favoured with our presence. In the glittering lights of that rendezvous of all the pleasures, we had gorged ourselves with champagne, lascivious dances, shouts and laughter.

The fabulously rich Cecilia Landhole, one of the prettiest women in New York, was there. So were the lovely Dolores del Monte, the wife of a Brazilian planter, Daisy Spanling, the wife of an automobile manufacturer and, finally, an unknown but ravishing girl from Ziegfield's Follies, whose name was Clara.

As for the men, there were four of us: Bob Walsley, the American journalist, Jim Berton, an industrialist, an Argentinian style gigolo, who we had picked up during the course of the evening and, of course, yours truly.

This travelling party was being held in my honour. I had known Bob Walsley for a long time, and he had invited me in order to acquaint me with the nocturnal pleasures of New York.

It astonished me to see how easily women of the very highest society accepted the presence of a simple chorus girl like Clara, upon whom they had never set eyes before that evening. But in America, when one goes on the spree, there are no longer any social classes, only drunks and women anxious to make love.

'Why don't we go to Clareb's?' Bob proposed suddenly at about two o'clock in the morning.

Immediately all the women's eyes lit up.

'Oh, yes!' they exclaimed. 'Let's go to Clareb's.'

The establishment in question was not like the ones we had previously visited: here there were no crowds, no noisy jazz, no dancing. It was what they call a 'speakeasy', that is to say an all-night restaurant. There was nothing there but private dining rooms, and it was in one of these that we installed ourselves.

The cosy room was well-furnished and bathed in a propitiously soft light. A few lamps with pink shades, comfortable divans in every corner and, in the centre of the room stood a table surrounded by some chairs.

Bob ordered champagne, a lot of champagne, while we seated ourselves, like sensible, well-bred people, at the table.

Like most Frenchmen, I can hold my drink, especially champagne. In spite of the enormous quantity of the stuff which I had already imbibed, I still had my wits about me. But one could not have said as much for my three companions. The women, although they were not so drunk, were in a highly excitable state. Their eyes sparkled, they laughed noisily, throwing themselves back in their chairs, and it was obvious that something was going to happen which would be a fitting climax to this orgiastic night.

Clara, the chorus-girl, was the one who set things going.

A gramophone standing unobtrusively in a corner of the room had just started to play a very popular melody.

'That's one of the tunes we dance to at the Burlesque!' she exclaimed joyfully.

Immediately she stood up, climbed onto the table and started dancing for us. Her little feet in their golden lamé shoes trampled the roses which were strewn on the cloth. They executed the dainty steps of the dance among the classes of champagne without overturning a single one.

I contemplated those perfect legs, which were so close to my face, and felt my virility stiffen. It seemed to me that a heady perfume emanated from under that swirling skirt.

The rhythm of Clara's dance became wilder. She whirled round and round; her skirt rose up from time to time, giving us tantalizing glimpses of lovely white thighs and red silk suspenders.

Still dancing, the girl began to disrobe. Her dress fell in an airy corolla about her ankles. She stepped out of it, with a kick, sent it flying across the room.

All she was wearing now was a little pair of pink silk knickers, trimmed with lace. The young woman wore neither slip nor brassière; her naked breasts were full and firm and the bright red of the thrusting nipples indicated that they had been rouged.

I could not take my eyes off that slender dancing form. Clara wriggled her hips seductively. The thin silk of the knickers clung to those plump moving buttocks. Nothing could have been more suggestive than those two globes of flesh encased in the tight silk!

All the men were looking lustfully at that bottom and I could tell from the expression in their eyes that they were as aroused as I was.

When at length Clara returned to her seat, it was easy to measure her success by the rather tight-lipped

123

look of the other women. Obviously, they were feeling jealous; they too wanted to be admired.

Suddenly Cecilia Landhole stood up.

'You're quite right, Clara,' she said. 'It's so hot here!'

As she was speaking, the young woman's nimble fingers were unfastening her evening-dress which slid down to her feet. That aristocratic American lady's curvaceous, sculptured body was then revealed to us clad only in a tiny black lacy brassière and black silk knickers, which revealed more than they concealed two magnificent buttocks.

'What a good idea!' exclaimed Dolores enthusiastically.

She quickly slipped off her clothes too. Soon everyone could see that the lovely Brazilian lady was not wearing a chemise and that her knickers were of white silk, agreeably decorated with red ribbon.

Daisy Spanling needed no further encouragement. She too removed her dress, revealing that she was clad in the most diaphonous lingerie.

Everyone continued to drink but now, quite obviously, champagne was no longer their main preoccupation. The men were all tremendously excited by the near nudity of the ladies and looks were being exchanged which were full of promise.

Without any more ado, Bob Walsley put his arm round Daisy's slender waist, then leaned forward and their mouths met in a long, passionate kiss.

'Hey, that's not playing the game!' cried Dolores, half annoyed, half amused. 'He's my partner, Daisy!'

'Why is Bob your partner?' retorted Daisy. 'No one here has got an official partner.'

'She's quite right, you know,' said Cecilia, laughing. 'But perhaps we ought to . . .'

At that moment, Bob Walsley slapped himself noisily on the forehead.

'I've got it!' he cried. 'We'll play a little game! It'll be great fun! Here's what we'll do: the ladies go out of the room for a moment and unveil their charming posteriors. Then they hide themselves behind this curtain so that all we men can see is that particular part of their anatomy. Then each man chooses his partner by looking at what is thus revealed!'

'That's a jolly good idea!' the ladies exclaimed, clapping their hands together excitedly. Then they went into an adjoining room to prepare themselves.

Meanwhile, Bob hung the tablecloth over the half-opened door in such a way that it formed a narrow gap with the curtain: thus the ladies would be able to show us their buttocks without revealing anything else.

'Right, girls! We're ready!' Bob called.

We could hear muffled laughter as they moved into position. Then suddenly, four naked feminine posteriors appeared in the gap between the tablecloth and the curtain.

'You choose first,' Walsley said to me.

I looked gravely at the row of bottoms. I had already recognized all of them. My eyes lingered on a particularly white, almost boyish rump, which undoubtedly belonged to the lovely Daisy Spanling.

Right beside it, a more insolent behind stuck out. The provocative roundness of the buttocks, the warm brown complexion of the skin proclaimed that this was Dolores del Monte's posterior.

Its neighbour had to belong to Clara, our dancer: magnificent buttocks, but without an ounce of superfluous fat, whose powdered, slightly pink flesh evoked the music-hall.

125

But the most lovely of all those bottoms was incontestably Cecilia Landhole's: nothing could compete with such generously plump white buttocks, so admirably well-shaped, tempting as ripe fruit!

I gave it a familiar tap with my hand.

'I choose this one,' I said.

'Charmed, Monsieur Frenchman,' a happy voice responded. 'Cecilia Landhole's derrière is extremely honoured!'

The game continued. Jim Berton, the industrialist, chose Daisy Spanling's aristocratic rump. The young man of Argentinian appearance favoured Dolores del Monte's imposing behind. Finally, Clara's buttocks fell to Bob Walsley.

'Now we've all got partners, let's have a good time!' the journalist proclaimed.

He put out the lights and opened the window. Discreet moonlight provided the only illumination in the little room.

I settled down on one of the four divans and I'm sure the others did the same.

'Where's the Frenchman?' said Cecilia.

'Here!' I replied loudly.

Almost immediately, a nude form glided towards me. The American woman's magnificent body pressed itself against mine, while two warm lips sealed mine in a long, passionate kiss.

The propitious twilight was soon filled with voluptuous sighs and groans. That only increased our desire.

In next to no time I had divested myself of my clothes and pulled Cecilia's satin-smooth body to me. My hands were exploring every part of that lovely nudity. After having lengthily caressed the soft, swelling breasts, they descended to her hips.

126

My exploring fingers probed between the young woman's thighs and were soon stroking a hot, wet furrow.

Cecilia was panting, her head resting on my shoulder. I went on fingering her, preparing the way, while she gasped and panted ever more loudly. At length, when I judged the time to be right, I penetrated her. She cried out as my rigid organ slid into the slick, warm depths.

Close to us, Dolores cried out:

'Take me, darling! Take me!' she said.

On all the divans, naked bodies were writhing in a communal dance of lust. The warm darkness was filled with the soft cries of women and the deeper moans of men.

The moonlight revealed imprecise white forms embracing each other and moving spasmodically.

I possessed Cecilia with intense passion and when she exhaled her pleasure in a great cry, similar cries came from the other divans, like so many voluptuous echoes.

Later on, we changed partners. When Cecilia had gone, Dolores del Monte approached me in the shadows.

She caressed me long and skilfully and her cool fingers soon restored my virility, then she bent forward and took my rigid length into her mouth. It was not long before the young woman's tenacious expert sucking brought me to the very height of pleasure.

I met Cecilia again the following day. In accordance with my promise to myself, I got her to agree to meet me for three more nights. We explored every facet of love, including those which are forbidden.

But my most vivid memory is of our first night,

when our lovemaking took place in the midst of all those other couples.

Hawaiian Pleasures

Hawaii . . . the poetry of the Islands, the local colour, made up of nostalgia, of languor and voluptuousness, all of which seems made for love without bounds, for eternal love.

I had become acquainted with one of the local girls, a dancer, who was the star attraction in an open-air cabaret. She had the fine features of her race, darkly abundant springy hair, a rather flat nose, which did not in any way detract from her charm, immense black eyes and a sensual mouth.

The young woman had a body which was brown and supple, with well-rounded breasts crowned by prominent nipples, and her legs were long and slender.

She danced in native costume: that is to say with bare breasts, clad only in a grass skirt and a tiny pair of silk knickers. A wreath of white flowers crowned the girl's head, while another one hung round her neck, descending as far as the waist.

She spoke English, which facilitated our relationship. I shall spare you a detailed description of that first evening of which the only really interesting part was the girl's dancing.

To the accompaniment of Hawaiian guitars, in the blue spotlight of a projector, she frenziedly mimed the act of love. During that wild dance, she whirled and wriggled and writhed like a snake, while her little face contorted itself into the most astonishingly pathetic expressions.

Then the rhythm diminished in intensity. The guitars sobbed like animals wounded by love. The dancer followed that suggestive music with her whole body. She arched her back, moving her hips as if she was making love. It was very impressive. She panted in the throes of that imaginary coupling. Her breasts seemed to swell, her nipples stiffening with the voluptuousness of the dance. The young woman's bottom moved suggestively under the grass skirt. Legs parted, she succumbed to the night's embrace, sinking to the ground intoxicated with desire, while the guitars sobbed out their melody.

Wild applause greeted the end of that dance. Smiling, pleased with herself, the little lady came and sat down at my table. I had already invited her before the dance began.

She was called Loula and couldn't have been more than seventeen or eighteen. Loula was a perspicacious girl, so she realized immediately how much her performance had affected me. Far from being upset by that fact, the young woman found it absolutely natural: in Hawaii love is as normal, as easily attainable as eating and drinking.

She took me to her bungalow, a nice little place, with a big picture window looking out on the sea.

She came and sat down on a mat beside me, a pretty little woman ready to do whatever I desired.

In fact, I sensed such a ready compliance in her that I found it somewhat offputting; however, this did not stop me from caressing her breasts. That simple contact was enough to reawaken my flagging desire.

Never in the whole of my amorous life had I handled such exquisite breasts! They were not large, it is true, but they were so beautifully shaped and fitted so well into my hands! They were like two velvety fruits; I could feel the nipples growing stiff as I caressed them.

Loula moaned and pressed herself close to me. When I tried to kiss her on the mouth, she wouldn't let me but insisted that I should begin with her forehead, in accordance with tradition. It was a pleasure to obey the lovely girl's wishes, so I planted a quasi-paternal kiss on that warm, smooth forehead before pressing my lips to hers.

She responded ardently, with a voluptuous sigh. Meanwhile, my fingers were busy unfastening the grass skirt. Then they started to explore the little silk knickers. It was not long before they were caressing the girl's hairy mound through the thin material.

These activities were having a quite dramatic effect on me: my organ was so stiff by now that it was almost painful!

At length, I pulled her knickers down and she made no attempt to stop me.

Quite naked now, Loula crouched between my thighs then started to caress my rigid sex with her fingers. She ran them up and down the entire length with a firm but gentle touch.

I was filled with delightful sensations. The sweet perfumes of the night came through the open window and stars scintillated in the sky. Plaintive sounds from a distant guitar formed a fitting accompaniment to our increasing desire.

Then Loula's mouth replaced her hands. With a skilfulness which I have never encountered before nor since, she kissed my throbbing length, finally taking

131

it into her warm wet mouth and sucking it until I was on the point of coming.

When she realized that my climax was imminent, she withdrew her mouth, smiled at me affectionately, then knelt on all fours in front of me.

I found myself gazing at the softly rounded globes of the girl's buttocks, a very enticing sight! Then she used her fingers to open the lips of her sex, thus indicating what I was to do next.

No words were necessary. I slid into that wet welcoming passage, while Loula moved her bottom artfully to increase my pleasure. As I moved in and out, she murmured a stream of melodious words in her own language, which were accompanied by the distant chords of the guitar. I was in a happy state of sensual intoxication. Nothing mattered but that hot slick sheath which clasped my length so firmly yet so sweetly! Never have I encountered another woman who knew how to wriggle her bottom so delightfully!

I was on the point of coming when Loula suddenly disengaged herself. For a moment I was really angry, not understanding the reason for such an interruption. But the little lady rolled over onto her back and pulled me between her open thighs.

That warm welcoming femininity soon swallowed me up again. She was getting wetter and wetter, then she was in the throes of orgasm! The young woman came silently, without any other sound than that of her panting breath, bottom moving frenetically, sex palpitating; then I came too, spurting the liquid evidence of my passion into Loula's warm depths.

For more than an hour we lay on the mat, resting in each other's arms. The guitar was silent now, the stillness of the night was broken only by cries of nocturnal birds.

That was my first experience of love in Hawaii. It was unpretentious, lively and imaginative.

After three more nights, which were equally enjoyable, I took my leave of the pretty dancer and set out on my travels again.

Chinese Pleasures

I staggered out of a bar, very much the worse for drink. The humid night air enveloped me, heavy and stifling. I felt as if I was going to be sick. There must be better ways to pass the time!

I had spent the whole evening in a somewhat less than respectable bar surrounded by a noisy crowd of people whose features and forms were indistinct in the murky atmosphere. How many drinks had I consumed? That question is impossible for me to answer. But it was too many, that's for sure!

I had fallen asleep for a time, back there in the bar. It was a wonder that some villain hadn't picked my pocket!

Now, my sole desire was to get back to the hotel, take some aspirin and get to bed.

I walked unsteadily along a narrow, badly-paved street. The doors of every home were open, forming rectangles of pale light in the darkness. In each doorway stood a slender woman, perfectly still, looking out for prospective clients.

I passed by several of these ladies of the night without paying them any attention. But suddenly one of them came to my notice and I couldn't take my eyes off her.

She was an adorable little Chinese woman, with a

dainty but well-proportioned body. An elaborate edifice of shiny black hair, decorated with tortoiseshell combs, crowned her charming features. The young woman's eyelids were decorated with blue mascara. Her mouth was bright red and well-shaped. Her hands and feet were very small, very white, with long carmine nails.

A sudden desire to make love to this pretty Chinese woman took possession of me. She realized what I wanted and stood aside in order to let me enter. She gave me a respectful bow.

The woman followed me into the room then with light, obsequious gestures, helped me to undress. I felt her active little hands brushing against my body as she helped me. All her movements were extremely graceful and delicate.

I watched her face as she removed my clothes: it remained passive, dignified.

Soon I was completely naked, then the doll-like Chinese girl sprayed strange perfume all around me. Then, armed with an oddly shaped bottle, she poured an odorous oil into the palm of her hand, with which she proceeded to anoint the most intimate parts of my body.

Was it some property of that oil, or the effect of those delicate fingers? Anyway, I was filled with a bizarre sense of voluptuousness and my organ stiffened into full erection.

As if that was what she had been waiting for, the little Chinese lady knelt in front of me, then started to kiss my virility with soft, warm lips. After a while, the lips were replaced by an agile tongue, which ran up and down my throbbing length, giving me most delightful sensations. At the same time, her hands were stroking my buttocks.

She kept this up for about half an hour, which passed very quickly, so pleasing were those subtle kisses and that tongue! It seemed to me that a thousand butterflies were tickling me with their satin wings. The strange thing about it was that while the young woman kept me in an almost painful state of arousal, she never brought me close to an orgasm. I nearly begged her to bring me off as she knelt there alternately kissing and licking.

At length the delightful torture ceased. Standing in front of me, the strange girl started to undress.

It didn't take long, for she wore nothing but a kimono fastened around the waist by a silk orange-coloured sash. In less than no time she was naked, revealing her beautiful, fragile body to me without any false modesty.

We lay down side by side and her cool fingers played with my genitals.

She moved down to my feet and began to lick them like a submissive slave-girl. Her tongue tickled me delightfully as it caressed my toes. I was filled with a marvellous sense of voluptuousness!

Then she started to move upwards, kissing my thighs, belly and chest. Suddenly, her pretty little face was hovering over mine and she was licking my face with her pointed tongue. That tongue licked my nose, my lips, my eyelids – even my ears!

Meanwhile, the young woman's body pressed itself close to me: I could feel her warm belly against mine and her small but perfectly rounded breasts were crushed against my chest. I managed to slide down under that slender body and take one of the breasts into my mouth. The Chinese girl gave a little cry of pleasure. I started to suck upon the nipple, which

136

grew harder as a result of the stimulation. It was oily and tasted of bitter almonds.

At length, the young lady sat astride me. I was lying on my back and didn't have to make the slightest effort. She literally impaled herself upon my rigid weapon, then started to move up and down upon it.

As she moved faster and faster, I was afraid of hurting the fragile creature. But although her body was small, her love-nest was big enough to accommodate me easily. The young woman's face remained impassive but from time to time she uttered tiny cries.

Suddenly she took my head in her hands and pressed her lips to mine in a long kiss which tasted of peppermint.

At the moment of orgasm, she detached her mouth from mine, then gave a harsh cry. The slant eyes closed and she went very still, gripping my flanks tightly between her thighs.

A few moments later, the girl got up in order to make some tea. She brought it to me in a tiny cup and offered it to me in a kneeling position.

I murmured my thanks and sat there feeling very grand. While I drank the tea, she sponged me down, then dried me with a large towel.

This new way of making love was far from displeasing to me. I returned to the little courtesan on three more nights and every time she satisfied my desire with subtle caresses which no Western woman would have been able to offer.

Parisian Pleasures

Duvernier was silent. His two friends, who had been listening to him with passionate interest, suddenly came back down to earth.

'Is that all?' said Gontran de Longuelade.

Jacques laughed.

'It seems to me that it's enough,' he said. 'What more do you want?'

Chauvelard relit his pipe for the twenty-fifth time.

'My dear chap,' he said, between two puffs, 'what you have told us is damned interesting! In each of your stories you have vividly depicted a different woman. And I must admit that your love-life shows a great deal of variety!'

'Tell us,' said Longuelade, 'of all those women, English, Spanish, American, Hawaiian, Chinese, which do you prefer?'

'The sixth!' replied Duvernier gravely. 'The lady I have known for only a few days but who I already consider to be the most complete: a Frenchwoman!'

And as his friends looked somewhat surprised, he continued:

'Yes, I must admit that I know very little about Frenchwomen. I have done so much travelling that I have spent only a few months in France; however, a few days ago I met what seems to me to be the ideal woman.

'Oh, she's not a Princess, nor a fabulously rich adventuress seeking strong sensations, nor a waitress, nor a prostitute. She is a woman who works, like many others. She has all the good qualities of the Frenchwoman: intelligence, a happy disposition, courage, industriousness without too much ambition, sensivity and a romantic nature, which is so delightfully feminine!

'You will say that I am chauvinistic, or in love: you're probably right on both counts . . . but I assure you that none of the women I have been telling you about represented my ideal woman, even though they were all exceptional in their way and were delightful companions.

'No, there is no doubt about it, the greatest pleasure I have had has been in Paris, but you must forgive me for not being too frank this time. One thing must be made clear, however: Parisian pleasures are not just the orgies in the Bois de Boulogne, where half-drunk girls are pawed about by dissolute bankers while voyeurs look on . . . neither are they to be found solely in the crapulous night-clubs of Montmartre, where one pays five hundred francs for a bottle of champagne . . .

'Parisian pleasures are also the minutes of delightful expectancy when one is waiting for a pretty girl to finish work, the time one spends with her in a pleasant restaurant on the banks of the Seine, or huddled together watching a silly film in a cinema.

'Parisian pleasures are also those wonderful moments when one holds a pretty girl in one's arms and feels her body quivering with amorous voluptuousness . . . They are the exquisite moments

139

when she gives herself to you, not seeking complex or perverse satisfaction, but simply because she loves you and wants to be part of you . . . Those are the true Parisian pleasures!'

Duvernier fell silent. Chauvelard nodded his head.

'You're undoubtedly right,' he murmured. 'And have you found such a woman, truly?'

'I think so,' Jacques replied, smiling. 'I have only spent four nights with her, but I know that I want to spend another night with her and many many more after that!'

It's a simple enough story. The girl in question is twenty and she works as a mannequin in a big fashion house. You are undoubtedly aware that among mannequins there are two categories of women: those who use their profession to get themselves into the world of wealth and luxury, and whose greatest ambition is to hook an elderly moneybags. But the second category is made up of girls who earn their living without 'going to bed,' or who at least seek only the pleasure of the senses or the sentiments when they take a lover.

Josianne belongs to the second group. It was quite by chance that I met her.

I was accompanying a friend, a Brazilian lady, to a great fashion house.

The monotonous presentation of the models, the seemingly endless parade of mannequins with their insipid smiles soon bored me to tears. I was so restless that I discreetly detached myself from my Brazilian friend, who was too absorbed in considering the relative merits of the different outfits to notice anyway, and wandered along some corridors.

140

Suddenly, from behind a velvet curtain there arose the sound of joyful feminine chatter and laughter.

My curiosity was aroused, so I approached the velvet curtain which, by some fortunate chance, had a gap in it wide enough to permit an indiscreet observer to see what was going on without being seen himself. The temptation was too great to be resisted!

In a brightly lit room, three ravishing young women were talking and laughing: they were undoubtedly mannequins. One was very tall, with dark brown hair and beautiful green eyes; her very made-up face had a rather vulgar appearance. She was smoking a cigarette, perched on a table, legs crossed. All she wore was a short pink slip, from which long shapely legs emerged sheathed in silk.

Another pretty girl with black hair and an equally shapely figure was standing up, legs apart, hands on hips. She wore nothing but a tiny tulle brassiere and a dear little pair of pink silk knickers which moulded her bottom and her sex.

The third girl stood at the back of the room listening to the other two. Her beauty particularly impressed me: she was a radiantly lovely blonde, with clear blue eyes and full red lips: a true daughter of France, tall, generously proportioned, with frank, cheerful features.

'My lover always has me from the rear,' the tall dark-haired girl was saying in a loud voice.

'That doesn't surprise me at all,' replied the girl on the table, 'not with a bum like yours!'

'It's no bigger than yours!' the other replied, obviously vexed.

'Let's have a look.'

The dark girl turned round, exhibiting her generous bottom, tightly encased in pink silk.

141

'Oh, with your knickers on you can't really tell,' said the brunette banteringly.

'But of course you can! Look!'

And the mannequin pulled the knickers tightly across her bottom. The silk moulded the two round buttocks perfectly, clearly revealing the deep cleft separating them. In that way, her behind appeared to be bare, while that pink covering gave an added suggestiveness to it.

When she had sufficiently exhibited her derrière, the girl turned round.

'It's your turn now!' she said.

Nonchalantly the brunette descended from the table, then raised her slip. A pair of big buttocks sheathed in brief white silk knickers appeared. But the lovely girl didn't stop there: she pulled them right down and they lay in a fragile heap around her ankles. They were generous buttocks with very soft white flesh.

The dark-haired girl shrugged.

'There's not much difference,' was all she said.

She turned to the blonde who, so far, had not uttered a word.

'And what about you, Miss Butter-Wouldn't-Melt-In-Your-Mouth? Are you going to show us your bum?'

'You can go and take a running jump!' replied that young lady calmly.

Her two companions laughed contemptuously.

'The virtuous Josianne!' jeered the brunette. 'Why can't you be natural?'

It's probably not worth seeing anyway!' said the dark-haired girl. 'But all the same, we'll have a look!'

She turned to her ally.

'Let's give her a spanking. That'll teach her to put on airs!'

142

They both advanced on the girl who backed away, looking quite pale.

'Don't you dare lay a finger on me!' she said nervously.

But the girl with the green eyes had already leapt upon her imprisoning poor Josianne's wrists, while her pal pulled the young woman's skirt up.

A charming derrière appeared, sheathed in pale blue silk. Contrasting pleasingly with the very white flesh of the thighs, matching suspenders supported sheer silk stockings, a charming spectacle!

But at that moment, there was the sound of someone approaching in the corridor. The girls immediately released their frightened victim. As for myself, I judged it prudent to withdraw and strolled back to the salon, trying to look as if nothing had happened.

Shortly afterwards, the lovely Josianne appeared modelling an evening-dress. While my friend was involved in a discussion with the head seamstress, I was able to approach the mannequin and murmur a few sweet nothings in her ear, as well as asking if she would like to have an aperitif with me later. But she only shrugged her shoulders indifferently.

However, I was bent on making the young lady's acquaintance, cost what it may. So when it was time for the shops to close, I drove over to the fashion-house and parked my car not far from the main entrance, then waited for the employees to emerge.

Soon, a large crowd of pretty, laughing salesgirls flooded out into the street. I spotted Josianne walking away with rapid steps. I got out of the car and ran after her, finally accosting the young woman in the most vulgar fashion, asking her to go with me to a nearby bar! Ah, my friends, what a business! She came pretty close to slapping my face. At last, however, by dint of soothing and persuasive words, I succeeded in getting her to agree to meet me following day.

She turned up. I will spare you the details of our first date. Suffice it to say that I strove to show myself at my very best: sentimental and tender. Never before had I spoken to a woman with such fiery eloquence, and perhaps sincerity. The little lady was moved. It was obvious that she found me pleasing. I realized that she was full of the warm sentimentality of youth, a tenderness which longed to express itself.

We met again the next day and every day for the following week, but only for an aperitif. At the end of that time, she agreed to spend a whole evening with me.

It was a simple but charming evening, which began on the terrace of a restaurant on the banks of the Seine, then continued in the friendly shadows of a cinema. The little mannequin's eyes gazed at me expressively. I sensed that I had succeeded in winning her confidence and her heart.

Finally, we went to a dance-hall. The excitement and the champagne had brought a flush to the young woman's cheeks and a sparkle to her eyes. To be honest, until then I had given no thought as to what I intended to do. Josianne pleased me greatly, there was no doubt about that, but I didn't really know whether I loved her.

Certainly I desired the lovely girl intensely and it was that more than anything else which prompted me to suggest that we should go to my apartment.

When I had opened the front door, she hesitated before entering. But the charm of the evening still

144

cast its spell over her. She stepped inside like a little bird, nervous lest it is entering a trap.

When we were in my bedroom, Josianne suddenly seemed to wake up to what she was doing and wanted to leave immediately. I realized that if I tried to insist that she stayed, there would be a very real risk of losing her for good. I began to tell the young woman how I felt about her, using the most gentle, the most tender words.

By this time she was sitting on my knees, the warmth of that lovely body penetrating mine.

Our lips met in a long voluptuous kiss. Soon our tongues were exploring each other's mouths.

Next, my hands began gently to undress her. First of all I undid the buttons on the top part of the dress, then slid it down together with the silk slip underneath. Smooth white shoulders appeared, then two warm round breasts crowned with red nipples. When I leaned forward and began to kiss them, the little lady gave a soft cry.

I took one of the nipples into my mouth and began gently to suck it, as well as part of the breast around the nipple.

Josianne was so aroused by this time that she raised no objection when I took her dress right off. She was now wearing nothing but a pair of pink silk knickers. Her face was buried in my shoulder and my hands were caressing the young woman's body: one of them was stroking the smooth buttocks under the knickers.

I don't remember exactly how we got rid of the knickers. Josianne, intoxicated with voluptuousness, had closed her eyes. Naked and languishing, she let me carry her to the bed.

I undressed rapidly then lay down beside her. At

the contact of my body she opened her eyes wide in alarm.

'No, we mustn't!' she said. 'Listen . . .'

But I was not listening. I was too busy covering her lovely body with ardent kisses. Josianne sighed and occasionally tried to push me away, but without much conviction. Finally, she just lay back and surrendered to pleasure.

'Jacques,' she murmured, 'my darling Jacques.'

She wound her arms around my neck. I was so aroused that my throbbing organ was almost hurting me!

For some moments I had been gently stroking her sex and titillating the clitoris in order to excite Josianne and prepare her for penetration. She was very wet. Her breath was coming in short gasps.

Then I got between the young woman's thighs. The swollen head of my organ brushed against her thatch of pubic hair.

'Jacques, darling,' she gasped, 'I love you!'

Banal words, a cliché, but at that moment they seemed to me to be the loveliest words in the world!

Then I coated the tip of my weapon liberally with saliva in order to facilitate entry. Next, parting the little lips of Josianne's sex, I put myself in position and started gently but firmly to push in.

'No, darling . . . No!'

So I stopped for a moment, whispering tender words of encouragement to my beloved.

When she relaxed I tried again, but it was not easy and several times it was necessary to stop in order to avoid hurting her unnecessarily.

But then, just when I was near to relinquishing my efforts, something gave way, Josianne cried out like a little wounded animal, and my rigid organ slid all the way in. Josianne was no longer a virgin!

During the next few mintues, I did everything possible to efface any memory of pain, to overwhelm her with pleasure. Gradually, Josianne began to respond with increasing passion, moving her hips in time with mine. As we made love, the young woman whispered tender words in my ear.

Gasping with newly-discovered pleasure, she moved her hips seductively, which greatly increased my enjoyment. There was an expression of voluptuous tenderness in her eyes.

Casual affairs no longer had any attraction for me. I had found something far more worthwhile!

Josianne gave herself to me simply, without any sophisticated tricks. And I realized that as well as giving me her body, she was offering me her whole being, the love of an innocent girl!

When I reached the moment of supreme pleasure, inundating the young woman with my ecstasy, she cried aloud and clasped me tightly and told me how happy I had made her.

For a long time afterwards we lay there with our arms around each other, lost in the same dream of voluptuous love. The darkness surrounded us like a heavy perfumed blanket. Josianne's fresh breath mingled with mine. Sometimes her body quivered and her arms clasped me more tightly.

It was a delicious languor, all the more delightful for me because it was without complexes.

And I assure you, my friends, that when, a little later, Josianne fully realized what had happened and said, with tears shining in her eyes, 'Promise me that you won't stop loving me,' that was perhaps rather naive, but it was also something else, something wonderful: the gift of a pure heart after giving me an untouched body.

Since then I have come to realize how fortunate I am. Josianne has spent the past four nights with me, four passionate nights at the conclusion of which every morning has found us exhausted but incredibly happy at finding each other.

She is the most sensitive of mistresses and has a strange perspicacity as far as caresses are concerned: what I call a sense of love; she is sensual but unselfishly so and her kisses are imbued with the most exquisite tenderness.

What is so moving is the simplicity and the spontaneity which she brings to our relationship. I realize now that if I need these so much, it is because I had forgotten their existence.

And if I travel again in the future, it will be with Josianne by my side. Then, when we return, I shall be able to tell you about something else: the love of a French lady in the different countries of the world!

Epilogue

Duvernier's head was bowed as if he was thinking deeply. Chauvelard stood up and shook his pipe.

'In short, my dear fellow, you've been hooked!'

'Yes,' said Gontran, 'like an inexperienced youth!'

Jacques was too preoccupied to notice the rather jealous irony in the words.

'It's true,' he said, shrugging his shoulders. 'I can't deny it. I've been "hooked", as you say, but what of it? Haven't I had the happiest of lives? My fortune has enabled me to travel a great deal. I have loved love and savoured its delight in many different countries. I have recounted several of my most striking experiences to you. And it is not just empty boasting to say that I have had many other adventures, as you've probably guessed.

'But this is the most serious one of all: the one which I hope is going to terminate my career as a womanizer in the best possible way.'

'If I understand you correctly,' said Chauveland, 'the Englishwoman you told us about was a hypocrite, the Spanish girl unbridled, the American woman vicious, the Hawaiian facile, the Chinese venal, the French girl perfect . . .'

'Well,' said Jacques, 'setting aside Josianne's case, which for me is something quite different, have I not managed to combat the theories of our friend, Gontran? You maintained, my dear fellow, that all women resemble each other in bed. Come now, honestly, when I was telling my English story didn't you discern the astonishing prudery of that nation, which only permits sensuality when it is legal? And in the case of the Americans, the need for vice supported by dollars in the nocturnal life on Broadway, as well as abroad? And didn't my Spanish girl cry out a love which was typical of her country: earthy, fiery, hot and sunny? Not to mention the Hawaiian girl, who expressed the facile pleasures of a land blessed by Eros, nor the Chinese lady whose dainty, submissive gestures are the heritage of a tradition which is a thousand years old.'

Longuelade removed his monocle.

'You're right, my dear fellow,' he said. 'I bow to your superior perspicacity.'

'I say, old chap,' said Chauvelard as he rose to his feet, 'all these stories you've told us would make an excellent book!'

'I'll have to think about that!' said Jacques with a laugh.

The night was already coming to an end, giving way to to the dawn whose pale pink mists could be seen through the windows.

Then, having nothing more to say to each other, the three men separated and returned to their respective destinies.

Jeanine
(extracts)

'Jeanine' first appeared in the autumn of 1957. It is not properly speaking an erotic novel but a psychological study of the effects of war upon a young couple; however, it contains a number of scenes of a very explicitly erotic nature and these got the publisher into trouble with the authorities and led to the book being withdrawn only a few weeks after its publication. A new edition appeared in the spring of 1958 with the offending passages deleted.

The following extracts comprise some of the passages which were omitted from the 1958 edition.

This is the first time that any part of the novel has been published in an English translation. The story takes place in occupied France in 1943. Jeanine is an attractive young war widow living in a small provincial town.

Jeanine lay in the darkness of the bedroom waiting for sleep to overtake her. But sleep was slow to come: it was so hot and stuffy! The window was open but that didn't seem to make any difference: there was not the faintest stirring of a breeze.

She'd never been able to get used to sleeping alone in the three years since her husband had disappeared.

God, how she missed him! Not that she had ever really been in love with him, but it was nice to have someone beside you in bed and, whatever his faults

153

may have been, Georges certainly knew how to make love to a girl!

She remembered the fuss he used to make of her breasts – how he would fondle them, kiss them, greedily sucking at the nipples until Jeanine was reduced to a trembling jelly of voluptuous longing. Then he would climb between her widely spread thighs and push his long stiff thing right up into her . . .

Now the memory of all that was stirring the young woman's desires – desires which for so long had not been satisfied. Her fingers were stroking her moist sex-lips and the sensitive clitoris as well.

But at that point she stopped thinking about Georges: it was a fantasy which now absorbed all of Jeanine's attention . . . The young man had come to her in the still of the night, like an incubus conjured up by her frustrated longings. She couldn't quite recall his features but just knew they must be young and handsome.

She remembered how the mysterious stranger had climbed between her open thighs, how easily his erect penis had slipped into her.

Now Jeanine's fingers were working furiously and she was gasping and panting. She thought of the way in which the stranger's hairy testicles bounced against her white buttocks.

'He's fucking me now!' she gasped. 'He's fucking me with his big cock!'

And as she uttered these words, the young woman came, inundating her fingers with a gush of warm fluid.

That evening before she went to bed, Jeanine took off

all her clothes and stood naked in front of the long mirror in her bedroom.

There was no perceptible swelling of the belly yet, of course, but her breasts were getting bigger, that was undeniable. They were large, very white and soft, with a thin tracery of blue veins running through them. The dark pointing nipples which formed their tips had become very sensitive lately.

Being nude like that in front of the long mirror always made Jeanine feel sexy, probably through association because that same mirror had played an important role in her sexual relations with Georges.

Goodness, the number of times that, at his instigation, she'd stood naked, gazing at her own reflection in the long mirror while Georges, also naked, stood behind her fondling the young woman's breasts with one hand while with the other one, he groped between her thighs! At such moments, she would feel his long stiff member prodding at her buttocks.

Memories like that were calculated to stir the senses of a healthy young female who had been deprived of a proper relationship for more than three years. Jeanine's nipples stiffened and she felt a delightfully voluptuous sensation between her thighs.

She knew that it was wrong but couldn't resist the feelings which were overwhelming her; remorse would come later!

She sank down into an easy-chair and with those long, elegant legs draped over each of its arms, started to masturbate.

The young widow remembered how nice Georges' stiff penis used to feel as it slid in and out of her wet vagina . . . Sometimes she would kneel on the floor in front of the mirror and he would take her from behind, his hairy testicles swinging back and forth.

At other times he would sit on a chair while she sat on his lap, impaling herself on his rod of flesh, then Jeanine would move up and down, faster and faster, breasts bouncing wildly, until they both achieved an orgasm.

God, how lovely that had been! Now, however, she was a poor girl all alone and had nothing but her fingers with which to try to achieve release.

'Georges!' she gasped. 'Oh Georges, fuck me with your lovely stiff prick!'

Then she came, once again inundating her slender fingers with a warm flood.

But it could never be as good as the real thing . . .

I gazed at Jeanine as she slept. She was lying on her back on the eiderdown: not under the bedclothes, but on top of them and because it was so hot, she wasn't wearing anything at all.

How lovely she looked lying there in the pale moonlight which poured in through the uncurtained window. A real live, erotic Sleeping Beauty, with long fair hair, just like the princess in the fairy tale!

Her pubic hair was fair too . . . fair and fleecy, nestling between plump white, slightly parted thighs.

The large breasts, flattened out because of the supine position of her body, rose and fell regularly: they were crowned with prominent dark nipples.

My member stiffened up, filling me with desire. Big breasts crowned with large nipples always have that effect on me.

But what I was also finding even more exciting was the sight of that sex, which seemed to be offering itself between the parted thighs. I could clearly see the lips through the light covering of downy hair.

My virility was as hard as iron now and throbbing with the intensity of desire.

A crude word came into my mind – it was the word 'cunt!' I don't usually employ such terms but at that moment voluptuous feelings were surging through me, banishing inhibitions.

Looked at in retrospect, however, everything which happened between Jeanine and me that night has acquired a dreamlike quality, in spite of the crude lustfulness which had me in its spell. Undoubtedly the moonlight played no small part in creating such an atmosphere.

I don't really remember getting undressed: perhaps my garments just fell away! Nor do I recall moving from the door to the bed . . . Perhaps I just floated there! But I do remember sitting on the bed beside the sleeping woman and placing my hand between her thighs! She stirred restlessly, mumbled incoherently, then lay still again. Her love-nest felt delightfully soft and warm.

I moistened my forefinger with some saliva and stroked the young woman's sex-lips, then titillated the little button at the top where they joined. Again she stirred and grunted but did not wake up, nor did she close her thighs.

In fact, there were so many signs that she found what I was doing far from disagreeable that I began to suspect that the young lady wasn't really alseep at all!

As my fingers continued to play with her sex it got wetter, her stomach muscles kept contracting and she was breathing hard. Perhaps she was having an erotic dream! 'Anyway,' I thought, 'the lady's ready for a good fucking!' So without any more ado, I climbed between those open thighs and penetrated the sleeping girl.

My rigid member slid easily into that warm wet passage. Jeanine sighed and moaned softly as I moved in and out, backwards and forwards with increasing vigour.

Unfortunately, it couldn't last long, for I was far too excited. After only a few more thrusts sensual pleasure overwhelmed me: my sperm gushed forth in long spurts as if it would never stop. That was one of the most intense orgasms I have ever had. Deeply satisfying!

Then it was all over; I withdrew and slumped down beside Jeanine, breathing heavily.

I became conscious of a hand gently stroking the hairs on my chest and Jeanine's voice brought my already drifting thoughts back to reality.

'Was that nice?' she enquired, in the soft, seductive tone which was one of her most pleasing features.

I opened my eyes: she was leaning on her elbow against the pillow, smiling down at me.

I stretched my hand out and gently stroked the lovely girl's cheek.

'It was wonderful!' I said fervently.

Jeanine smiled with pleasure at the compliment, conscious no doubt of the sincerity in my tone.

'Men are such strange creatures!' she said. 'Why do I always have to pretend to be asleep?'

'You don't *always* have to,' I replied.

'I do quite often,' she said.

'You don't mind, do you?' I said.

The young woman smiled tenderly at me. 'No, I don't mind,' she murmured and snuggled up close to me. We fell asleep in each other's arms.

There is a certain irony in the fact that at a time when thousands of people were suffering terrible hardships and dying all over Europe, my worst experience should have been attending a three-week course for officers at Auxerre, which was about a hundred and thirty kilometres from Combrai, and Jeanine!

In the six weeks since the beginning of our liaison I had become terribly attached to the dear girl and to be suddenly deprived of her company was the cruellest of tortures.

Unfortunately, attendance at the course was obligatory: there was no possibility whatsoever of getting out of it, so I had to spend three miserable weeks at Auxerre.

Luckily the demands of the course kept me fully occupied for most of the day, or else I think I may well have gone crazy. The worst thing was being alone in my quarters at night: then loneliness and frustrated desire would come to torment me . . .

Lying there on my narrow army bed, I would remember how pretty Jeanine was, how elegantly she dressed, what an excellent companion she made.

Then because my instincts were those of a healthy young male animal, my mind inevitably conjured up more intimately erotic memories: the way Jeanine's breasts quivered when she moved about the house wearing nothing but a thin silken dressing-gown; the elegant nonchalance with which she would hitch up her skirt and adjust a recalcitrant suspender; the incredible white softness of the young lady's bottom cheeks, which wriggled so seductively when she walked; the dark, mysterious valley that separated those round buttocks; the way she would lie there on the big double bed after we had made love, thighs still wide apart, semen oozing from between her half-open sex lips to form a damp patch on the sheet . . .

All of these titillating images invariably proved too much for me and always ended up in the same manner: that is to say with me furiously rubbing my stiff prick until I spattered seed all over my belly.

Then remorse would come to haunt me: I would feel ashamed, believing that by succumbing to such an adolescent practice, I had somehow let Jeanine down. I resolved not to give in to temptation again, but two or three nights later the same thing would happen once again.

Luckily, however, the course soon came to an end and I was able to return to Combrai and my beloved Jeanine.

When we arrived at Jeanine's house, she made some coffee, then we took it into the living-room and sat on the sofa, with a little distance between us, to drink it.

As we sipped from elegant blue and white china cups, we chatted in a friendly enough way about the wedding, her sister, the other officers who had been present at the ceremony and various other matters.

Judging from the warmth of her manner when she was speaking to me, it seemed clear that Jeanine had forgiven me for my previous misdemeanour. I felt sure that, with time and patience, I would be able to win back the sweet girl's love.

Indeed, she looked particularly attractive that evening in the soft light shed by a lamp with a pink shade which stood in a corner of the room. She had had her hair done the previous day and it looked very nice, falling in soft fair curls to her shoulders. Her face was carefully made up and she was wearing small blue pendant earings which were the same colour as her eyes.

I had noticed how admiringly my brother officers had looked at Jeanine at the reception that afternoon. She really did look lovely in the simple but elegant blue dress, which she was still wearing.

I moved closer to her and took her hand in mine. It felt soft and warm and I could smell the musky perfume which the young lady was wearing. My penis began to stiffen up expectantly.

'I want to make you happy, Jeanine,' I said, quite sincerely. 'And I want to make amends for any unhappiness you may have experienced because of my selfish behaviour.'

'I know, Heinrich,' she murmured, and her beautiful blue eyes were warm as they looked at me.

Then I took my new wife in my arms and kissed her tenderly upon the lips. She just remained passive at first, then gradually began to respond until we were kissing passionately, exploring each other's mouths with our tongues.

I helped Jeanine to remove most of her clothes and in no time at all the lovely girl was practically naked: she was wearing nothing but a mauve suspender-belt, a pair of sheer stockings and dark-blue, high-heeled shoes.

By that time we were both standing up and I was fondling and kissing my wife's superb breasts. They seemed even larger than I remembered them, large but beautifully-shaped! The prominent dark nipples were stiff and pointing, indicating how sexually aroused the young woman had become as a result of our love-play.

I too was in a state of sexual arousal: my penis had

161

grown rock-hard, but I was determined not to be too hasty in my love-making.

Jeanine gave a sharp intake of breath when my fingers touched her sex. It was very wet and the clitoris was rigid. The young woman glued her mouth to mine in a passionate kiss as I started gently to masturbate her. But almost immediately she pushed my hand away and gasped, 'No, Heinrich, not like that!'

Her hair was delightfully dishevelled, her cheeks were flushed, her eyes shining.

Then she helped me out of my trousers and pants and I stood there in the middle of the living-room with my penis sticking out like a flag-pole. Jeanine looked at it appreciatively then made me sit down on a straight-backed chair.

'I just want to . . . ,' she started to say, but never finished the sentence, for at that moment the young woman sat down on my lap facing me, legs astride, at the same time impaling herself on my stiff prick!

What an exquisite sensation to feel oneself engulfed in that hot, slippery sheath between a woman's thighs!

For a few timeless moments the lovely girl just sat there, eyes closed, savouring the feel of me inside her, then placing her hands on my shoulders for support, she began to move up and down on my rigid tool, at the same time kissing me passionately upon the mouth.

Up and down she bounced, gradually getting faster. It was a memorably erotic experience to be fucked like that by a hot naked woman, eager for love!

Lewd feelings and crude words surged through my mind but I didn't dare say them aloud for fear of offending Jeanine. (It was not until some time afterwards that I found out that my wife liked to use crude words when making love.)

162

'What a hot little slut she is! Ooh, what a lovely deep twat!' Those were some of the unuttered thoughts passing through my mind as Jeanine rode me. One of my hands was fondling a plump breast while the other was gripping a smooth bottom-cheek.

Then suddenly I was in the throes of orgasm. My semen spurted into that wet, wide-open vagina: it spurted and spurted until my testicles were drained dry.

Never had I had such a deeply satisfying fuck!

Unfortunately, Jeanine had not achieved an orgasm, so it was necessary for me to satisfy her with my fingers. But that was all right . . . It is only in erotic novels that couples come simultaneously, with a machine-like precision. I am writing about two human-beings!

The exciting events of the day, followed by such passionate love-making had exhausted us, so we went to bed and after exchanging a few tender kisses and caresses, we fell asleep with our arms around each other . . .

Irene

You have asked me to write about my most exciting erotic experience. Well, I'll do my best to oblige you, but it must be said at the outset that few men can have had a more uneventful life in that respect.

It is true that I have been married to the most charming of women for more than thirty years, but our sexual life has always been pretty conventional and unexciting; besides, it would be very bad taste on my part to expose our intimate life to the public gaze.

In fact, I have only ever had one really exciting erotic experience: it was the one and only time when I was unfaithful to my wife and although far from equalling the exploits of Casanova, at least it has the merit of being absolutely true.

What I am about to tell you took place in a small town in the south of England more than twenty years ago. Forgive me for not being more precise, but it is possible that the lady, and her husband, might still be alive and I should not like to cause them any pain or embarrassment. For the same reason, I have changed the lady's name.

At that time, I had recently graduated and was just starting on my teaching career. My intention was to spend a year working in an English school in order to improve my command of the language. I had no difficulty in obtaining a post as an assistant French master in a state secondary school situated, as has already been said, in a small town in the south . . .

The job was quite a pleasant one; the classes were large but my pupils were reasonably well-behaved and gave me no trouble most of the time.

I had been married for a little more than a year, but Catherine – my wife – had not accompanied me to England: she had an excellent job in a bank in our home-town of Nemours and as we were saving up to buy a house, we agreed that it would be best for her to remain in France and keep working. Besides, as she didn't speak English she would have been very isolated: so we decided to make the best of it for a year.

That was all very well but, of course, neither of us took into account the disastrous effets that such a separation was likely to have upon our physical and psychological well-being. A year doesn't sound very long, but when one is young and healthy and suddenly deprived of the pleasures of the flesh . . .

Certainly it would be true to say that no one could have suffered more than I did from the deprivation of those pleasures! As time went by my frustrated longing grew . . . I was never one to make friends easily and the fact that I was so often on my own, outside of school hours, only served to make matters worse.

The only erotic consolation available to me was a small but select collection of novels: *Dom Bougre, Les joies de Lolotte, Le roman de Violette,** etc. I had brought these with me from France and found some

---

* All available in modern English translations from the publisher.

168

comfort in reading them, for they were extremely well-written and contained many very titillating scenes.

I also possessed a few very explicit photographs that came from a shop in Soho and which had cost me a small fortune. They showed a couple making love in various positions: he was a short, thickset, balding man of about forty with a lot of coarse hair all over his body; she, however, was a very pretty young woman with attractive curly brown hair. Both of them were completely naked, except for the very high-heeled shoes worn by the young lady.

There were five photos in the set. My favourite was one in which the man lay on his back on a bed while the woman knelt beside him sucking his penis: you could see her shapely white bottom quite clearly and the man had his hand between her thighs playing with her sex.

The number of times I sat in my lonely bed-sit masturbating as I gazed at that photo, wishing it was my stiff penis in that warm, wet sucking mouth!

Masturbation as an alternative to regular love-making can be very enjoyable, but as a long-term substitute for the real thing, it leaves much to be desired. I had become accustomed to having sex with a warm, passionate, responsive woman and making love to that photograph definitely did not satisfy me: I longed for female company. In short, I was ripe for a spot of adultery.

An opportunity for committing that particular sin soon presented itself in the person of a young woman named Irene Elmwood.

Irene was the mother of one of my pupils, a twelve-year-old boy called Gerald, and I first met her at an open evening at the school towards the end of the spring term.

She was a dark-haired, petite woman with elfin features and an execrable taste in dress which immediately appealed to me: that evening, for instance, she wore a pink nylon blouse through which one could clearly make out the shape of her breasts and nipples; her white skirt was much too short as well as being too tight, so that one could see the outline of her knickers as she walked and, completing this vulgar ensemble, the young woman's slender legs were sheathed in sheer dark nylon stockings while her feet were encased in white high-heeled shoes.

I found the lady irresistible! In fact, all the time she was with me that first evening I had a tremendous erection! And there was little doubt in my mind that Irene found me attractive too, for she was sending out all those signals which women usually give forth when they want to encourage a man's advances: soft words, smiles, admiring glances, etc.

I met the delectable Mrs Elmwood again a few days later when I cycled into the town to have my lunch at a little restaurant where the food was good and not very expensive.

She was cycling too, in the opposite direction. We stopped when we saw each other and got into conversation. She told me that she was on her way home after doing a bit of shopping. I told her about my intention of having lunch and asked her to do me the honour of joining me. To my delight, she accepted, so we went off to the restaurant together.

Irene was a working-class girl, obviously unused to eating in restaurants: she seemed embarrassed when we arrived, but her pink-cheeked confusion only added to her charm as far as I was concerned. However, after we had ordered the food, she relaxed a bit and we had a most enjoyable meal.

I enjoyed talking to her: she put me at my ease, made me feel self-confident, protective. In fact, the young woman's company pleased me so much that I made up my mind to spend the afternoon with her instead of going back to school!

At first, Irene tried to dissuade me from doing such a thing, but my mind was made up and, anyway, she wanted sex as much as I did, so she soon gave up.

We decided to cycle out into the country, where we would be away from people. It was a pleasant sunny afternoon, quite warm enough for making love out of doors!

We went into a small wood on the outskirts of the town and soon found a little clearing which suited our purpose admirably.

That day Irene looked particularly attractive in a fluffy pink jumper, a very tight grey skirt, which was of course too short for good taste, and she was again wearing sheer dark nylons but with red high-heeled shoes this time.

We sat down on the grass together, whereupon I immediately took the lovely lady into my arms and started kissing her. To my delight, she didn't draw away but responded with great ardour. It wasn't long before we were exploring each other's open mouths with our tongues, then one of my hands was inside her jumper fondling a small but well-formed breast crowned with a large, stiff nipple.

By that time my member had become rigid and it throbbed with almost painful desire. This was much better than making love to a photograph!

I withdrew my hand from Irene's breast and placed it on a smooth, nylon-clad thigh; then I moved upwards until I was stroking the warm flesh above the stocking top; then I slipped my fingers under the elastic of her knickers and started to caress a vagina whose wet, gaping warmth showed how ready the lady was to perform the act of love!

In fact, we were both breathing hard, both eager to consummate our passion. When I started to pull Irene's knickers down, she helped me by raising her bottom so that I could pull them right off.

They were exquisitely fragile pink things, eminently suitable to protect such a treasure as nestled between those snowy thighs! I slipped them into one of my pockets, then I unzipped my trousers and took them off.

What followed next was one of those technical incidents which can be very distressing for both partners at such a moment: my erection disappeared! My penis, which until then had been proudly erect, went limp and nothing I did could persuade it to stand up again. I held Irene in my arms, fondled her breasts, then fingered her wet, burning sex, but all in vain!

Of course, she soon realized that something was wrong; however, she was very kind to me and used various stratagems to revive my flagging ardour, such as caressing my limp organ, tickling the testicles and nibbling the lobes of my ear. When these failed to do the trick, the lovely girl sat up beside me, then bent forward and took my penis right into her delightfully warm wet mouth. It was the first time that anyone had ever performed fellatio on me and I nearly fainted with pleasure. Never had I experienced such exquisitely voluptuous sensations! Irene sucked me with an expertise which proved very effective, for within a matter of seconds my organ was stiff again and throbbing with desire.

Then she withdrew her mouth, lay back down on

the grass and pulled up her skirt, showing me a pretty little love-nest framed between delicate white thighs.

'Come on, love,' she said, 'fuck me!'

I needed no further invitation. I got between those thighs, which opened wide to welcome me, and slid into that hot slippery passage as easily as a knife goes through butter. It felt lovely there, right up inside Irene's vagina; we just lay there for a few moments, kissing and embracing, enjoying the sweet sensation of being joined together.

But soon, impelled by the desire for ultimate satisfaction, I began to move my rigid penis back and forth. Irene moaned with delight and immediately began moving her bottom in time with my thrusts.

Heavens! What joy! Even now, all these years later, just thinking about it gives me an erection!

In and out, back and forth I went, faster and faster, gasping, red-faced with my exertions. Irene's love-passage was so juicy that it kept making squishing sounds as the swollen tip of my member plunged in after each partial withdrawal.

I think she'd already come two or three times. Certainly she made a great deal of noise, gasping, moaning, sobbing and saying things like, 'Oh yes, darling! Fuck me! Go on, fuck me with your lovely big cock!' I found such an uninhibited enjoyment of sex madly exciting.

Suddenly she said, 'Come on, darling, give it to me! Fill me with your stuff!' and I felt her cool, slender fingers tickling my scrotum.

That did it! I came immediately, shooting jet after jet of sperm into Irene's hot wet depths. It seemed to go on and on but came to an end at last, then I collapsed in a panting, sweating heap on top of my

173

companion, which is the sort of inconsiderate thing young men do when their desires have been satisfied.

'Ooh, you're heavy, love!' Irene said in an uncomfortable tone of voice after a few moments. I mumbled an apology and withdrew.

We lay there for some time talking. We got on well together, quite apart from sex. Late afternoon sunlight shone through the trees and the only other sound, apart from our voices, was the song of the nesting birds.

Looking back with the wisdom of hindsight, I can see now that it was one of those idyllically happy moments whose rarity makes them so precious, but at that time I was too young, too foolish to appreciate it.

An absurd, an odious sense of pride filled me, distorting my view of the situation and preventing me from enjoying Irene's company, from appreciating her as she deserved. I had recently been reading that great erotic masterpiece, *Les Liaisons Dangereuses*, and was identifying myself with its libertine hero, the Vicomte de Valmont. 'I have triumphed! I have conquered her!' I was thinking, or words to that effect. Could anything have been more ludicrous?

It must have shown in my manner, there's no doubt about that, for although we did it one more time that afternoon, and although we met two or three times afterwards for meals or walks, we never made love again.

Poor Irene! Instead of becoming the object of my gratitude and affection, she found herself confronted with a pompous young fool who behaved as if he owned her! No wonder she showed no desire to repeat the experience!

There is an epilogue to this tale . . . a tail to the tale, as it were.

I left England in the summer of the following year and did not see Irene Elmwood again for twenty years.

A few weeks ago, Catherine and I had to spend a few days at Boulogne because her mother, who lives on the outskirts of that seaport, was seriously ill. Fortunately, however, the old lady recovered and we were able to return home to Nemours, but before doing so, we spent a pleasant day shopping in Boulogne.

At about one o'clock that day, as the weather was fine, my wife and I were sitting on the terrace of a restaurant having our lunch.

We had not been there long when two women arrived and sat down at a table fairly close to us. I recognized Irene straight away, although the years had not been kind to her: the once attractive dark hair was now lank and streaked with grey; her face was quite haggard-looking. As for the unfortunate woman's clothes, flamboyant vulgarity had been replaced by drab mediocrity. I felt terribly sad for her sake. 'Tyme, cruel tyme,' as an Elizabethan poet said.

Irene's companion was very much younger: in fact, she couldn''t have been older than about eighteen or twenty. I guessed that the young lady was Irene's daughter, for she had the same elfin-featured prettiness that her mother had possessed twenty years previously, but her hair was not so dark and she had much better taste as regards clothes.

My former mistress had not noticed me, for she was deep in conversation with the girl. I would have liked to go across and speak to her, but Catherine's presence made that impossible.

My wife's voice broke in upon my thoughts: 'She's pretty, isn't she?' she said.

'Who?' I replied, knowing perfectly well who she meant.

Catherine smiled maliciously: 'The English girl, of course. You've had eyes for no one else for the past few minutes,' she said.

'As a matter of fact, it's the older woman who I've been looking at,' I replied.

'Oh yes!' said Catherine.

'Yes,' I went on, undaunted by my wife's incredulity. 'The lady's face is familiar . . . I'm sure I've seen her somewhere before.'

Catherine fell silent. Several times during the rest of the meal I noticed her eyes wandering in the direction where the English women were sitting.

Several hours later, when we were driving back to Nemours, Catherine said:

'Talking about faces being familiar . . .'

'A propos of what?' I asked.

'A propos of those two women in the restaurant,' she replied.

'Well?' I enquired.

'Well, it's very strange but the younger one's face seemed familiar to *me* . . . I've been trying to think who she reminded me of all the afternoon, and now I've got it!'

'Who did she remind you of?' I said.

'*You*,' Catherine replied. 'She reminded me of you when you were young.'

My wife's words struck me like a thunderbolt! I looked at her: the expression on her face was casual, unconcerned. She obviously had no idea of the gravity of what she had just said, fortunately for me!

'Did she really?' I said, not having to counterfeit the surprise in my voice. 'That is strange: as far as I know, I haven't got any relatives who are English.'

We drove in silence for a few moments, then Catherine said, 'People can resemble each other without being related. It does happen, you know.'

I breathed an inward sigh of relief.

'I'm sure you're right,' I said.

But as we sped along the route nationale towards Nemours, a great feeling of exhilaration filled my whole being. Catherine and I had had no children, but now I knew that *I* had a daughter, a beautiful daughter conceived one sunny afternoon in England twenty years ago.

Pick-up

She was sitting in a dimly-lit bar just off the Place de Pigalle when I first set eyes on her: an attractive, mature woman in her mid thirties with long fair curly hair, a full sensual mouth and clear blue eyes.

She was sitting on a high stool, right elbow resting on the zinc top of the bar, long nylon-clad legs crossed, the very short skirt revealing her stocking tops and a glimpse of suspenders. The young woman's dress was black, extremely décolletée and tight-fitting. My prick stiffened as I gazed at the deep cleavage between her breasts. A deep cleavage between snowy white breasts always has the most voluptuous effect on me!

I wondered if she was a professional. I don't usually go with members of the oldest profession, but this one had extraordinary charm.

It didn't seem likely that she was anything else, alone in a rather disreputable bar, quite heavily made up, and sitting on a high stool revealing her stocking tops in such a manner!

The lady became aware of my eyes fixed insistently upon her and returned my stare boldly. Then she gave me a charming smile.

I needed no further encouragement but walked over

to where she was sitting, then perched myself on the stool next to her.

There were a few people sitting at various tables but we were the only two at the bar, for it was still fairly early in the evening.

'Can I buy you a drink?' I asked somewhat shyly: shyness has always rather hampered my approach to women.

'No need for that, darling,' she replied in a low pleasing voice. 'You want to fuck, don't you?'

I must have looked a bit taken aback, for she laughed . . . a soft, musical laugh and continued:

'What's the point of beating about the bush? I've got something to sell, you're a prospective client. It'll cost you fifty francs: straight sex – nothing funny! But you don't look as if you're the type who'd want anything nasty . . . I've got a room just round the corner from here . . . What do you say?'

How could I refuse such an attractive offer from such an attractive woman? Fifty francs represented quite a lot of money for me, for my job was not all that well-paid, but how can you put a price on a really good fuck?

So I said, 'Very well. Let's go then!'

She picked up a short fur jacket and threw it over her shoulders, then we went out into the night.

The street outside the bar was ill-lit and there were very few people about, so I permitted myself some liberties as we walked: I put my right arm round her waist while my left hand gently caressed the girl's breasts through the black dress. They were big and firm; she wasn't wearing a brassière! My prick had become so stiff that it was difficult for me to walk properly!

We turned right into a narrow street where there

were a lot of seedy hotels catering mainly for prostitutes and their clients.

'Not far to go now, chéri,' said my companion.

She led me through the narrow doorway of a building whose red neon sign proclaimed that it was the 'Hôtel de l'Est,' then we were ascending a narrow flight of creaking stairs. The young woman led the way, giving me a lovely view of her bottom which swayed enticingly a few inches from my face.

Then we were in the bedroom, a pathetically shabby little room smelling of cheap perfume and casual sex.

I took the lady of the night in my arms.

'What's your name?' I asked her.

'Madeleine,' she replied. 'What do they call you?'

'Alain,' I replied.

'Well, Alain,' she said, 'it's time for you to give me my little present.'

I drew my wallet out of an inside pocket and gave her the fifty francs which were the price of her favours.

She took the money, with a softly murmured 'merci' and stuffed it into the large red handbag she was carrying.

'Madeleine is a pretty name,' I said.

'I'm glad you like it,' the young woman said, putting the handbag on top of a chest of drawers which was badly in need of a lick of paint. Then she quickly unbuttoned her dress, slipped out of it and draped it casually over the back of a chair.

Madeleine was naked now, except for a white satin suspender-belt, sheer black stockings and red high-heeled shoes. She had obviously put lipstick on her nipples which formed a pleasing contrast with the milky whiteness of her plump breasts. A pretty tuft of fair pubic hair nestled between the young woman's thighs.

I just stood there without thinking of undressing, just gazing in admiration at her naked loveliness.

'You're very beautiful!' I exclaimed.

'Thank you, kind sir,' she said, obviously pleased by my compliment.

Then she came across to me and helped me to undress. In no time at all I was naked as well.

Next, the lovely lady made me squat down over a bidet and thoroughly washed my genitals. Then, when she had gently dried them with a towel, she knelt down in front of me, took my already half-hard penis into her mouth and started to suck it with great expertise.

Words are inadequate to describe the delightful sensations I experienced as the young woman sucked my rigid tool. And as her head bobbed up and down, she used her fingers to tickle my hairy balls.

It was so delightful that it couldn't last long. Another few seconds and I wouldn't be able to stop myself from spurting into that warm, wet sucking mouth!

My loud gasps and groans must have warned her, for Madeleine stopped what she was doing and withdrew her mouth, leaving me standing there looking down dazedly at my stiff prick, which was wet and glistening with her saliva.

'Time to fuck, I think,' she said, going over to the bed.

The young woman climbed on to it then knelt on the eiderdown on all fours, giving me an explicit view of her large white bottom as well as even more secret charms.

She looked at me over a smooth round shoulder, gave me an enticing smile and said:

'Come on, darling, put that lovely stiff cock up me!'

What red-blooded man could refuse such an invitation? So I too climbed onto the bed, taking up a kneeling position behind her.

'What a lovely ass!' I thought as I contemplated the soft white globes of flesh. A dear little puckered reddish-brown eye peered up at me from the dark valley between them. I gently separated the buttocks with my hands so as to get a better view.

But Madeleine wasn't having any of that! She wriggled free saying:

'Now be a good boy! Put it in the proper place or I'm going!'

She sounded annoyed and I didn't want to upset her, so I directed my attention, and the swollen knob of my tool to the more customary portal.

Many years before, a friend had lent me a translation of *Memoirs of a Woman of Pleasure*, the famous eighteenth century English erotic novel and I realized that Madeleine and I had just enacted a scene from it: where Fanny discourages a sailor from entering her back door.

Anyway, there was no reason for me to regret Madeleine's refusal, for the young lady's cunt felt very nice; it gripped my prick firmly but gently. She was certainly giving me a good fifty francs worth, moving her hips artfully in time with my thrusts. A heady smell of perfume and sex hung in the air.

Then suddenly I was coming: there was no stopping it. In strong spurts I shot my semen into Madeleine's open cunt. It went on and on until my balls were empty.

When there was nothing more left for me to give, I withdrew from the young woman and lay down beside her to rest after so much excitement.

We lay there side by side talking for a while.

185

She was a likeable, intelligent girl – too intelligent to be peddling her ass in a bar in Pigalle it seemed to me. She talked interestingly about a number of different subjects.

I asked her if we could meet again.

She said: 'I'm always in that bar every evening between seven and midnight, except Sunday: that's my day off.'

I smiled and said, 'Never on Sunday, eh?'

She laughed, got off the bed then squatted down over the bidet. The sound of splashing water came to me.

It didn't take Madeleine long to get dressed, then she quickly repaired her make-up and ran a comb through her fair hair.

As she was about to leave, the young woman turned to me and said:

'Perhaps we'll meet again soon. You know where to find me . . . Bye!'

Then the door closed quietly behind her and she was gone.

I got up myself then, dressed quickly and left a few minutes later.

Less than an hour after that I was at home, sitting in a comfortable armchair listening to a jazz concert on the radio. I had had a shower and was wearing pyjamas and a dressing-gown. From time to time I took a sip from a glass of an excellent white wine. It had been an enjoyable evening. My encounter with Madeleine was very satisfactory. She'd drained me dry! If Brigitte Bardot had walked in and offered herself to me at that moment, I wouldn't have been able to do anything about it.

I'm not like the heroes of those pornographic novels

who can fuck twenty or thirty times in a night. No, I'm just an ordinary guy who can manage it usually about three or four times a week.

The jazz was good; so was the wine. A warm feeling of euphoria spread through me. I wondered if Madeleine had been fucked by anyone else yet.

The buzz of the doorbell broke in upon my thoughts.

I finished the drop of wine which was left in the glass and got up leisurely to see who it was.

What a surprise when I opened the door! Madeleine stood there, still wearing the tight black dress and her short fur jacket.

'What a lovely surprise!' I exclaimed. 'Come in, my dear,' and I stood back to let the young woman enter.

'Let me take your jacket.'

I helped her off with it then hung it up in the hall. Then we went into the living-room.

She sat down with a sigh on my Louis Quinze sofa, the only really decent piece of furniture I possess, and kicked off her red high-heeled shoes, then tucked her legs up under her.

'Would you like a drink?' I said.

'Please,' she replied. 'A glass of wine,' she added with a tired smile. I poured a glass and handed it to her.

'How was I tonight?' she demanded.

'Not bad. How was I?'

'Not bad,' she said with another smile, a rather ironical one this time.

'Well, that's all right then.'

I poured myself another glass of wine and sat down in the armchair facing Madeleine, or rather Estelle: 'Madeleine' is the name my wife uses when she plays the role of a woman of pleasure. We'd acted out this little play about the client and the prostitute five or six times now.

'We won't need to do it any more,' Estelle was saying. 'I think I've got the feel of the part now.'

'What a pity!' I said. 'It's been quite exciting really . . . When are you going to start the book?'

'Tomorrow, I think,' she replied. 'I've got more than enough material now.'

At this point perhaps I should explain that my wife is a moderately successful novelist and her latest idea was for a story about a respectable married woman leading a double life as a prostitute. It was Estelle's idea that we should act out a series of little scenes such as I have described in order to give her some idea of what it felt like to be a lady of the night.

Now she stretched luxuriously and yawned, then smiled at me coyly.

'I didn't come tonight, you know,' she said.

'Prostitutes aren't supposed to,' I replied. 'Not with their clients anyway.'

Estelle uncurled herself from the sofa and came over to me. She pushed my thighs apart, extracted my limp cock from the pyjama trousers, then took it into her lovely full-lipped mouth and started gently sucking it, using her tongue with great expertise.

Within a very short time my organ had stiffened up very satisfactorily.

Then she withdrew her mouth, looked up at me and said:

'I'm not really a prostitute and you're not my client. Come on, there's something I'd like you to do for me!'

Estelle stood up then walked towards our bedroom, her shapely bottom swaying seductively in the tight dress.

When she reached the door she turned and looked at me with a seductive smile.

'Are you coming?' she said.

'Not at the moment, but I reckon I soon shall be!' I said and followed my wife into our love-nest.

Something Unexpected

You may wonder exactly what I was doing wandering the streets at one o'clock in the morning anyway. Well, it would never have happened if Francine hadn't been so bloody-minded.

I'd been feeling randy all evening and when we went to bed, around half eleven, I started making up to her, feeling her tits and bum and everything. But she wasn't having any! No way!

I managed to pull her nightie up, but Francine's thighs were firmly welded together. Past experience should have taught me that it was useless to go on trying, but it's difficult to think straight with a hard-on. Perhaps if I'd been a bit more patient, a bit more tender, she'd have given me a hand-job (she's really very good at that). But you know how these things go: the first round ended with me saying something nasty and angrily turning my back on her.

But just try and bloody well sleep when you're angry and horny and your wife's lying there beside you stiff as a board with resentment, occasionally giving forth a muffled sob!

Anyway, round two opened with me having another go: I tried the tender approach this time, but it was too late for that. Francine pulled away from my caressing hands.

'Leave me alone!' she hissed. 'Go to sleep! All you ever think about is sex!'

That did it! I switched on the bedside lamp, got out of bed and quickly pulled some clothes on.

'Where are you going?' Francine said tearfully.

'Out!' I snarled; then I left the room, slamming the door behind me. I ran downstairs and out through the front door, slamming that too.

That's how I came to be wandering the streets at one o'clock in the morning.

We live in a quiet suburb so, not surprisingly, there was not a living soul about, apart from the odd tomcat in search of an erotic encounter.

A full moon hung in the sky and one could see everything as clearly as if it was broad daylight.

I wandered around for a while thinking about what a bitch Francine could be when she put her mind to it. Usually though she seemed to enjoy sex as much as I did, but she sometimes turned off cold, like tonight. Fortunately, it didn't happen too often.

Meanwhile, my rather aimless wandering had brought me to a small public garden, which was about a kilometre from where we lived. It was a pleasant spot in the heart of suburbia, with smooth well-kept lawns, flower-beds and a pond partially surrounded by trees at the centre.

There used to be railings and an iron gate which they locked at sundown, but the Germans took all that away during the Occupation, so now local couples could pop in there for a bit of quiet fucking after dark.

A woman was standing by the entrance to the garden. Naturally, it struck me as odd that she should

194

be standing there by herself like that in the small hours.

As I drew near, I could see her quite clearly in the double light of the moon and nearby street lamp.

The lady was a tall blonde: she wore an expensive-looking coat made of some kind of dark grey fur; her legs were sheathed in sheer dark nylon stockings, and she was wearing very elegant red high-heeled shoes.

As I came level with her, the woman smiled charmingly at me and said, 'Hello.'

She was not beautiful, not even pretty really, but an air of distinction, of refinement emanated from her, as well as a heady perfume. I felt my cock stir.

'Hello,' I replied.

The lady smiled again. 'It's a really beautiful night,' she said. Her voice was musical, cultured.

'It certainly is,' I agreed.

'Would you like to spend a little time with me?' she enquired.

Seeing my hesitation, she added, 'It won't cost you too much.'

'How much?' I demanded.

She gave me a long evaluating kind of look. Then, like a woman who has made up her mind that something is worth doing, she slowly pulled her fur coat right open and, to my delight, I could see that the lady was wearing nothing underneath it, except for a black satin suspender-belt, sheer stockings and high-heeled shoes.

Her face may have been ordinary but her body was exceptionally lovely: very slender, very white smooth skin, big soft breasts with prominent nipples which looked dark in the pale radiance of the moon.

My prick quickly stiffened into full erection!

'Well,' she said, 'how much do you think fucking me would be worth?'

'You're very lovely!' I said, with a sincere fervour which must have showed in my voice, for she smiled again – the lady really did have a quite uniquely charming smile – and held out her hand to me.

'Come on,' she said. 'We can talk about sordid things like money afterwards.'

And holding me by the hand, she led me into the public garden.

As we walked across the smooth turf towards the trees, the woman told me that her name was Mireille, that she was half Italian on her mother's side and that she came from Paris. I told her my christian name – Marcel – but judged it imprudent to mention Francine or our little difference of opinion.

When we reached the pond in the middle of the garden, she threw off her fur coat, carelessly letting it fall onto the damp grass.

I sat down on a wooden bench and gazed in admiration at my lovely companion. Her nudity had an unreal, almost dreamlike quality in the cold moonlight: with me sitting there fully-clothed and the pond and trees and everything, it must have looked like a scene straight out of one of Paul Delvaux's paintings.

Mireille came over and sat down on the bench beside me: it must have felt hard against that soft white ass! She put one arm around my shoulders while with her free hand she felt my swollen penis through my trousers.

'Goodness me! You are a dirty boy, aren't you!' she exclaimed in a soft, insinuating tone. 'I think you'd better unzip and let mummy have a look!'

With excited, fumbling fingers I hastened to comply

196

with her suggestion, revealing my stiff and with its swollen, mauve knob to the young woman's gaze.

'That's a lovely cock!' she murmured, stroking it with cool, well-manicured fingers.

Meanwhile, I was by no means inactive: I put one arm round her waist and stroked the warm flesh of the lady's hip, while with my other hand I caressed a firm thrusting breast. Mireille's tits really were marvellous – soft yet firm, if you know what I mean. The nipple grew stiffer as a result of my fondling. Our heavy breathing and the occasional hooting of an owl were the only sounds to be heard in the deep shadows cast by the trees. The moon's double floated in the silvery waters of the pond.

The fingers of my free hand were now busy between Mireille's thighs, which she had obligingly spread to facilitate my task. Her cunt was wet and open, the clitoris swollen and stiff.

'That's right, darling,' she gasped, breaking the silence, 'frig me . . . Oooh, that's lovely!' she moaned as I rubbed her clitoris.

Nothing could have been more exciting than to hear that cultured voice saying such things, to see a refined lady, who in the normal way would have nothing to do with the likes of me, reduced to such a state of panting desire! For, take it from me, Mireille had class, she really did!

As I continued to rub that hot, wet, gaping twat so her breath became more rasping and her language more obscene.

'Yes! Yes!' she chanted, 'stick your fingers up my snatch! Fuck me! Shag me! Oooh, I'm going to come!'

And she did just that, twisting and writhing on the hard bench, flooding my fingers with her hot love-juice. At the same moment my own orgasm hit me and I spurted semen all over my shirt. It was one of the best comes I'd ever had! And when it happened Mireille, too absorbed in her own sensations, wasn't even touching me!

After so much excitement, we had to rest for a while, so we just sat there for a few moments with our arms round each other.

Then Mireille stood up, stretched languorously, and went over to where her fur coat was still lying in a dark heap on the grass. When she bent down to pick it up, I had a delightful view of her generous ass. What a poetic sight! And what a poem I could write about it: I can already visualize the opening lines:

'Que je bande quand je vois
Un cul blanc et dodu
Luisant dans dans la nuit! . . .'*

All right, so it's not great poetry, not even good poetry, but what it lacks in talent it makes up for in sincerity. Anyway, it's not bad for a petrol-pump attendant!

And I've got good manners: I got up too and went over to Mireille and helped her on with her coat.

She turned to face me, gave me one of those charming smiles of hers, then said:

'About the money . . .'

I felt in the back pocket of my trousers and pulled out two rather crumpled fifty franc notes.

I offered them to her and said apologetically:

'That's all I've got on me, but you're worth much more . . . Look, why don't we meet again tomorrow? I'd really like to see you again and I'll have a lot more money then.'

* What a hard-on I get
When I see a plump white ass
Gleaming in the darkness! . . .

She took the notes, still smiling, and put them in her handbag. She said:

'All right. Same time, same place tomorrow.'

Then she gave me a light kiss on my cheek, turned on her heel and walked quickly away, leaving me standing in the little garden in the moonlight.

You're probably thinking what a dickhead I was to pay a whore when she hadn't even given me a proper hand-job, let alone a fuck but, believe me, I've had plenty of full-scale fucks which were far, far less exciting! It was no exaggeration to say that she was worth much more than a hundred francs.

When I arrived home a little later, Francine was flat out, snoring slightly. She didn't even stir when I got in beside her and it didn't take long for me to fall into a deep sleep as well.

The next night I was at the appointed place at the appointed time: the entrance to the little public garden at one a.m.

Luckily Francine had fallen asleep quite quickly, making it possible for me to slip out of the house without any trouble.

There were a lot of clouds in the sky tonight and the moon only appeared from time to time. Mireille was not there!

I waited and waited with rapidly diminishing hope. By two a.m. it was obvious that she wasn't going to turn up.

Then it occurred to me that she might be waiting down by the pond, under the trees: perhaps, in fact, she'd meant us to meet there!

With renewed hope and a beating heart I hastened down to the spot where we'd parted the previous night . . . , but she wasn't there.

I stood there feeling forlorn. At that moment, the moon appeared from behind the clouds and by its light I caught sight of something lying half hidden in a large clump of grass. I bent down and picked it up: it was two fifty-franc notes folded together!

What could this mean? Surely they couldn't be the notes I'd given to Mireille: I'd definitely seen her put them into her handbag. All the same, it was a strange coincidence. I put the money in my pocket and walked home deep in thought.

When I had undressed and was getting into bed, Francine stirred and said in a sleepy voice:

'Where've you been?'

'I couldn't sleep, so I went for a walk round the block,' I said, snuggling up to her. She came into my arms immediately: to my surprise and delight she was naked: I could feel her firm titties pressing against my chest – I always sleep naked, except on the coldest winter nights.

'I'm sorry I was such a bitch last night,' Francine said.

'And I'm sorry for being so nasty,' I said, kissing her tenderly on the forehead.

'It wasn't your fault,' my wife murmured. 'I just get into a mood sometimes; I don't know what comes over me.'

'Anyway,' she said, pulling away and sitting up, 'I know a way to make it up to you!'

'How,' I demanded.

She got into a kneeling position on the bed beside me.

'Like this,' she said and bending forward, she grasped my half hard tool near the base, took the

200

knob into her wet, warm mouth and started to suck it gently.

Any lingering thoughts about the puzzling business with Mireille were pushed out of my mind by the sweet sensations that sucking mouth was bringing me.

Within seconds my half hard-on had turned into a solid erection, filling Francine's mouth to capacity, but she continued to suck avidly, her dark curly-haired head bobbing up and down, faster and faster. I felt her fingers cradling my hairy balls and tickling them.

'Ooh, that's lovely!' I gasped. Drums seemed to be pounding in my ears: tum-te-tum, tum-te-tum, tum-te-tum. My cock had never been stiffer! I stretched a hand out and caressed Francine's soft warm buttocks.

Suddenly she stopped sucking me and knelt there beside me on the bed panting, mouth wet and slack.

'Don't stop!' I pleaded.

She smiled at me.

'Just having a breather,' she said. 'Don't worry, I'm going to make you come like you've never come before!'

Then the darling creature bent forward and took my prick back into her mouth and started to suck it again with renewed enthusiasm.

Meanwhile, I fondled her dangling tits, then played with her moist, half-open snatch. Feeling her love-hole like that was almost enough to make me come, but what finally did it was when Francine started to tickle my asshole with her finger. I couldn't resist that and I just exploded in her mouth: I spurted and spurted and spurted and I think she really must have been trying to please me, for she swallowed the lot! A thing she would never normally do.

They say the nice thing about lovers' quarrels is the

201

sweetness of making up afterwards; well, our reconciliation that night coudn't have been sweeter.

After she'd sucked me off, I sucked Francine's tits and played with her pussy until she had a lovely long come, then we went to sleep in each other's arms: there's no sleep so deep, so satisfying as that shared by two contented lovers. We were very happy!

For a few weeks I didn't really give much thought to my strange nocturnal encounter with Mireille. As it receded into the past it began to acquire a hazy, dream-like quality, like those Delvaux pictures I have already mentioned.

Then one day when we were tidying up the house, I came across something which gave me quite a shock.

Francine had got a big pile of old newspapers together to chuck out and I was just glancing through them, looking at the headlines and skimming through some of the articles, when on the front page of one of them I saw a picture of Mireille! Oh yes, it was her all right, there was no doubt about it.

The caption caught my eye, it said:

'Tragic Death of the Countess de Lamouran!'

Fascinated, I read the accompanying article, which went like this:

'Late last night, the Countess Anne-Mireille de Lamouran died instantly when the car she was driving collided with an articulated lorry near the Porte Maillot. The driver of the other vehicle only received light injuries.

'Countess de Lamouran, wife of Count Raoul de Lamouran, the industrialist, was well-known as a Parisian society hostess and also for her active work with various charitable organizations.'

The date on the paper was 30th May, 1949. Now

that shook me even more than reading about Mireille's death for, you see, my meeting with her took place towards the end of June, in the same year!

I can just see you shaking your head, disbelief written all over your face . . . And I can't really blame you! How could a woman whose death had been reported in the paper a month previously pick up a man and make love to him? And what was a wealthy, titled woman like Mireille doing picking up strange men and selling her favours? These are questions I have asked myself time and again and although I have come up with some answers, they can only amount to speculation.

I've never been inclined to believe in ghosts or the supernatural and, funnily enough, even this experience hasn't shaken my fundamental scepticism as regards such matters.

Most people's reactions whenever someone tells this kind of story, fall into one of two categories: either they display a frank incredulity, which is understandable but hardly flattering to the teller, or they immediately jump to the conclusion that it can only be explained in terms of the supernatural.

But readers of science-fiction will be aware of another possibility: what physicists call a spatio-temporal warp, I believe: what that means is that some parts of the space-time structure in which we live are vague, somewhat fluid, so that if you happen to be in the right spot at the right moment, you could find yourself actually living in the past, or the future for a while.

Far-fetched you say? Maybe, but is it any more far-fetched than believing that someone can come back from the dead?

The question why Mireille should have prostituted

herself is less difficult to answer. It is by no means an unheard of thing for bored society ladies to seek perverse thrills in such a way. She might, like Séverine, the heroine of Josef Kessel's remarkable novel *Belle de Jour* have been satisfying an irresistible masochistic urge to degrade herself. Or, like the Duchess of Sierra Leone in Barbey d'Aurevilly's tale *A Woman's Vengeance* she might have been getting back at a husband she hated. But of course, as has already been said, all of this is just speculation. The precise whys and wherefores will probably never be known.

All I know is that I long to meet the lovely Countess again! Often, when Francine is asleep, I slip out of the house and hang around the little public garden where we met that night. My hopes are always particularly high when the moon is full and the sky is clear.

I haven't seen her yet, but I'm certain she'll be there . . . one of these nights.

A Very French Love Story

They met every Wednesday in the hotel lounge and took morning coffee together.

He was forty-five, a rather slim, distinguished-looking man with brown hair greying at the temples. He possessed a small private income which he supplemented by translating as well as some other literary work.

She had once taught English in a lycée but had married a successful businessman and now devoted herself to music, literature, good conversation and making love but, as we shall see, not necessarily in that order.

Their names were Claire and Michel. He was married too, to an attractive woman, slightly younger than himself and who had achieved quite a good position in the civil service.

He would always be there at the hotel by ten, a few minutes before Claire arrived, so that he could savour the comfortable luxury of the surroundings and a pleasurable sense of anticipation.

There was usually some pleasant taped background music playing in the lounge: this morning it was one of his favourites – Schubert's lovely 'Trout' quintet. They both loved good music: it had been the thing which first brought them together – that and sex!

A young man approached and enquired courteously whether he would like some coffee. Michel replied that he was waiting for a friend to join him. The waiter smiled and withdrew.

Shortly afterwards Claire arrived, looking very attractive, as she always did on these occasions. She was a pretty woman with dark curly hair cut quite short. Her figure was on the plump side it is true, but he preferred that to the bean-pole skinniness which had become fashionable in recent years.

Michel stood up to greet her as he always did, clasping her shoulders and kissing her on both cheeks as if she were a friend or relative rather than his mistress!

Then they both sat down and Michel made a sign to the young waiter, who came to take their order.

'Coffee, please,' said Claire.

'Anything to eat?' the young man enquired.

'Croissants?' said Michel, raising his eyebrows at Claire.

She smiled, and it was like the sun coming out from behind the clouds.

'All right,' she said, 'but I shouldn't really!'

The waiter noted down their order, then went off to the kitchen for the coffee and croissants.

'I ought not to,' Claire repeated. 'I'm putting on far too much weight!'

'Nonsense!' Michel protested. 'You look fine!'

And he spoke nothing but the truth.

The morning being warm and sunny, Claire was wearing a most attractive yellow summer dress decorated with black circles. It was quite low-cut, giving one a glimpse of the deep cleavage between two soft white breasts. The fashionably slashed skirt had fallen away revealing smooth thighs encased in very sheer nylon tights. She also wore a pair of black high-heeled shoes and carried an elegant red shoulder bag made of real leather. Small red pendant earings hung from the lobes of her delicate ears. Her make-up was discreet, skilfully applied.

As always, Michel felt a rising sense of elation: Claire's presence invariably had that effect on him.

Their coffee, a large jug of it, arrived together with croissants, butter and jam. The waiter poured a cup each for them, then discreetly withdrew.

Claire took a sip from her cup and sat back with a sigh of contentment.

'This is nice!' she said.

' The music's nice too,' said Michel, putting butter and jam on his croissant.

'Oh, of course! "The Trout",' Claire exclaimed with a smile.

'I've more or less mastered the accompaniments to those Schubert songs,' Michel remarked as he bit into his croissant.

'Good! Perhaps we can have a go at them this Friday.' She bit delicately into her croissant.

'I'd love to!' said Michel with unfeigned enthusiasm.

As has already been said, they shared an enthusiasm for music. They had met on an evening course on Baroque music at the local university and had immediately struck up a friendship. They started going to each other's homes to make music together, for they were both excellent amateur musicians: he played the piano, while she possessed a fine contralto voice.

Of course, it wasn't long before they became lovers but, so far, neither Claire's husband nor Michel's wife suspected anything.

Another couple arrived and sat down at a nearby

table: she was quite a pretty, fair-haired young woman; he was a tall, good-looking man in his mid thirties with black hair. Both wore dark business clothes and carried brief-cases.

'Still reading Harriette Wilson?' enquired Michel, brushing crumbs off his knees.

Apart from music, literature was Claire's other main passion and her favourite book at the moment was *The Memoirs of Harriette Wilson*, the famous courtesan of the Regency period in England. Her husband had brought back a copy for her when he had visited that country on a business trip a few weeks previously.

'I certainly am!' Claire replied with enthusiasm. 'What a woman she was! She knew far more about the art of living and of being free than any of the so-called liberated women of today!'

Michel smiled indulgently at his mistress's vehement tone. He admired her lively personality, as well as desiring her body.

They continued to talk about Harriette Wilson and the elegant savoir-vivre which characterized those times while drinking their coffee and eating their croissants.

The couple at the next table were also deep in conversation, although what they were actually talking about might more justifiably be described as shallow rather than deep.

'Have you got the minutes of the A.G.M. with you?' she was saying in a rather inexpressive voice.

'No, unfortunately,' her companion replied in the same tone. 'But it was proposed that we should under-take a feasability study before committing ourselves too far.'

'Fine!' said the young woman. 'then we can talk about costing later.'

210

They were both so engrossed in their unexciting conversation that they were letting their coffee get cold.

At the same moment, Claire was saying, 'I can't understand why the English make so much of a prude like Jane Austen and so little of a real woman like Harriette!'

Michel gazed at her tenderly and said, 'I want to fuck you!' He said it in English, which they both spoke fluently. Claire blushed like a young girl and said, 'What, here?'

They both laughed happily at the thought of such scandalous behaviour. They each had a good sense of humour and neither of them made the mistake of taking life too seriously. Laughter and happiness were the essence of their relationship.

At the other table the man was saying, 'When do you think we'll be able to finalize the matter?'

'It shouldn't take longer than three weeks, I think,' the young woman replied. Even her drab business costume couldn't hide her essential prettiness.

Claire drank the last of her coffee and set the cup down. 'Shall we go?' she said.

'The usual place?' Michel asked, making a sign to the waiter.

'Not today,' Claire replied. 'Let's go to my place.'

Michel paid the bill and they left.

When they reached the street, he said, 'But you've always said . . . ,' and left the sentence unfinished.

'I know,' Claire replied, 'but today it's different!' There was a strange expression on her face.

Until now, their lovemaking had taken place mostly out of doors: they would drive out into the country, which was not far away, and do it in a pretty little clearing in a wood or on the banks of a winding river.

After all, it was summer and the weather was usually fine when they met; besides, Claire loved to fuck in the open air and always had satisfying orgasms when they did it in the country.

Once or twice, Michel had sugested that they should go to her place – he was rather less enthusiastic about the joys of rural fucking – but Claire had always been against it. What could have caused this sudden change of mind? he wondered.

She lived in an attractive modern bungalow on the outskirts of town. It only took them a few minutes to get there in Claire's little Volkswagen, which they always used on their expeditions.

Michel had been there two or three times in the evening when her husband had been at home: but that was to play music and be sociable – not to make love!

When they arrived, Claire parked in the gravel driveway in front of the bungalow. As he got out of the car, Michel couldn't help feeling a bit uneasy: he thought about nosey neighbours peering through their curtains and telling Claire's husband of his visit. He wished now that they had gone to one of their usual places, but Claire was a strong-minded woman and no one could resist her combination of charm and iron determination once she'd made up her mind to follow some particular course.

She opened the front door with her key then led him through the hall into the pleasantly light, airy bedroom which she shared with Maurice: this was situated at the rear of the bungalow.

The curtains were drawn and the filtered sunlight pervaded the room, enhancing its air of elegant comfort. They undressed in silence, then Claire went over to the window and peered through a chink in the curtains. The sight of his mistress's pale, soft nakedness drove all fears of possible discovery from Michel's mind. Oh, those smooth shoulders, that beautiful behind, those lovely long legs! His cock rose to the occasion and stood stiffly to attention. He came and stood behind the lovely lady, his hands cupping her full round breasts, his throbbing penis pressing against her buttocks. Michel's lips bestowed a shower of ardent kisses upon the nape of her neck, where the hair was very short and fluffy, and upon those-oh-so-white shoulders.

Claire sighed with pleasure then, letting the curtain fall back into place, turned to face him. She threw her arms around his neck and stood on tiptoe to give him a passionate, open-mouthed kiss.

Michel could feel two firm white breasts pressing against his chest. He put his hand between her thighs and ascertained how wet and warm she was down there: 'Ready for fucking!' he thought.

Claire's cool fingers cradled his hairy balls and caressed his penis for a few moments, then she murmured, 'Come, chéri,' and led him across to the big double bed.

She pulled back the elegant bright blue bedspread, then they both climbed onto the bed. They kissed and cuddled for a few moments but were both so ready that they were not inclined to delay their union.

Michel lay on his back, his erect member sticking up against his belly. Claire climbed on top of him, cocking her leg over his supine body, then reaching down, she grasped his tool and guided it into her eager love-hole. She closed her eyes and gave a long sigh of sheer happiness as she felt it enter her.

She leaned forward, putting her arms around his neck, pressing her cheek against his.

For a few moments they did not move but just lay there, savouring the pleasure of being united. Then clasping Michel's shoulders with her hands, Claire began to move her round white bottom up and down, but slowly, so as not to make him come too soon. Michel groaned with the exquisite sensations he was experiencing and grasped Claire's soft warm bottom cheeks in his hands; at the same time he separated them then gently fingered his mistress's tight puckered anus: he knew she loved that!

'Oh, yes,' she whispered, her breath hot against his cheek, 'play with my asshole!' Then she kissed him passionately on the lips.

It often amazed Michel that someone as refined and cultured as Claire could say such crude things when they were making love.

She was so excited now, her vagina was so wet that as his penis moved in and out it made a sort of splishing sound. This added to their excitement.

Claire's lovely behind was moving up and down quite fast now. Then suddenly she murmured in her lover's ear:

'Ooh, how I wish Maurice could see us fucking!'

This was something new: although Claire had often said crude things during their lovemaking, this was the first time she'd ever mentioned her husband at such a moment.

Michel by this time was too far gone to say anything articulate: he just moaned and gasped as his pretty mistress rode a cock horse on his rigid, glistening stem.

'I'd like him to catch us at it!' Claire gasped.

Her ass was moving up and down frantically now.

'I'd like to have your baby and pass it off as his!' Claire panted. As she uttered these profane words, her vaginal passage contracted in orgasmic spasms and she inundated Michel with a flood of warm liquid.

But before he could come too, his mistress slipped away from him, got up off the bed and went over to the window where she peered through a crack in the curtains, as she had done when they first entered the bedroom.

Understandably, Michel felt bewildered as well as frustrated. He pushed himself up on one elbow.

'What are you doing?' he demanded, a peevish note in his voice.

'Come and see . . . ,' she said, still peering through the narrow gap in the curtains.

Intrigued, in spite of himself, Michel got up and went across to join Claire, his now half-hard penis, still damp with her secretions, sticking out in front of him.

They stood together by the curtained window, both stark naked, and in a soft voice, almost a whisper, Claire said, 'Look!'

He put his eye to the chink, then got quite a shock, for Claire's husband, Maurice, was there in the garden!

Michel realized with growing dismay that he must have been there all the time that they'd been fucking on the bed, for he was sitting in a deck-chair going through some typed sheets, occasionally making amendments with an elegant gold-tipped fountain-pen: a man of about forty with receding sandy hair, spectacles and a rather florid complexion. An open brief case reposed on the grass near his feet.

Fortunately, Maurice was at the other end of the garden, at quite a distance from the bungalow, seated in such a way that his back was half turned to them.

Michel closed the curtains and turned angrily to Claire.

'Will you tell me what's going on?' he hissed.

Her only response was to press her warm naked body close to his, put her arms round him and press her full lips to his in a long, passionate kiss. Michel could feel the lovely woman's breasts and belly pressing tightly against him. His cock stiffened, his anger turned to desire. Michel's arms enfolded Claire; his hands stroked her firm back and swelling buttocks.

Then at last she broke the kiss and he felt her cool fingers stroking his cock. 'We must do something about this,' she murmured in a seductive tone.

She sank to her knees in front of him, then holding the stem near the base with her right hand, she slipped the swollen mauvish knob into her mouth and started to suck it enthusiastically, her dark head bobbing up and down.

Michel felt as if his knees were about to give way. Sweetly voluptuous sensations engulfed him: his whole being was centred in his cock, in that wet, warm cavern of delight!

Just as he felt that he was about to come, Claire withdrew her mouth and looking up at her lover with wide blue eyes, said:

'I wonder what Maurice would say if he knew that I was sucking my lover off only a few metres away from where he's sitting?'

Then, before Michel had time to react unfavourably, she slipped his tool back into her mouth and started to suck him again, her head bobbing up and down vigorously.

Suddenly, Michel felt her fingers tickling his hairy balls, then there was no holding back: he reached his peak and shot his semen into Claire's avidly sucking mouth in quick hot squirts, moaning with the sweet joy of release.

The dear girl swallowed every drop of the precious stuff: she didn't stop sucking until he had achieved complete satisfaction. Then she released his softening prick and looking up at him with shining eyes, said:

'There, now I've really been unfaithful to the bastard!'

As they drove back to the town centre a little later, Michel remonstrated with Claire for taking such a risk.

'Why did you do it?' he demanded. 'Supposing we'd been discovered?'

'Ah, but we weren't, were we?' Claire replied nonchalantly. 'As to why I did it – just let's say that the risk increases the pleasure. Don't you agree?'

She smiled at him, that radiant irresistible smile of hers, and Michel realized that she was right, that his relationship with her was a thousand times more exciting and rewarding then with any other women he had ever known and that he would fall in with anything she wanted to do.

'Of course I agree!' he said warmly, placing his hand on her knee and squeezing it affectionately.

He didn't know what Maurice had done to upset his wife; something had obviously gone wrong, but whatever it was he was on Claire's side, no matter what!

They pulled up in front of the hotel where they'd had their coffee that morning. Claire killed the engine. Then she turned to him, took his hand in hers and said:

'Do you remember the scene in *Madame Bovary* where Emma steals out of the house in the middle of

217

the night to make love to Rodolphe in the garden while her husband is asleep upstairs?'

'Who could forget it!' Michel replied.

'Well, I have a mind to play Emma to your Rodolphe,' she said . . . 'One evening next week, perhaps,' she added with a mischievous smile. 'When you've had time to recover from today's little escapade!'

'Well, we'll see what the weather's like,' said Michel. He was still worried by the idea of taking such risks. 'But it would be exciting, if we had a fine night,' he added, anxious to please his mistress.

He looked at his watch.

'I'd better be off,' he said.

He took her in his arms and kissed her long and tenderly.

As he was getting out of the car, Claire said, 'See you Friday then?'

'Yes,' he replied. 'I'm really looking forward to having a go at the Schubert!'

He slammed the door shut and Claire started the car. He waved to her as she moved away; she blew him a kiss.

Michel watched the car until it disappeared round a corner, then he set out to walk the kilometre or so which lay between him and his home, a pleasant old two-storey house situated in a residential district on the edge of the town. He always walked home after these rendezvous with Claire, feeling that the fresh air and exercise did him good.

That afternoon, as he walked along enjoying the warm sunshine, Michel went over in his mind what he and Claire had been doing: fucking in the conjugal bed with Maurice only a few metres away in the garden! He was half appalled, half excited by the audacity of it.

He remembered what Stendhal had written about one of his heroines: 'She had too ardent a soul to be contented with the realities of life,' and thought how exactly this description fitted Claire.

Dear Claire! Crazy, adorable Claire! She was right, of course: the element of risk, of being discovered increased the excitement immeasurably. He never felt more vital, more alive than when he was with her.

And now this mad idea about enacting a scene from *Madame Bovary*! Would he have the courage to do it?

A vision of Claire coming towards him under a starry sky, wearing nothing but the flimsiest of night-dresses, came into his mind. He would take her warm, perfumed body into his arms; she would press her soft lips to his and he would fondle her full, gently thrusting breasts . . . Michel suddenly had difficulty in walking and realized that when the time came, he *would* have the courage!

It was necessary to stop and look in a shop window for a moment in order to give his erection a chance to subside. Then, as Michel stood there looking unseeingly at the window display, another vision came into his mind of himself slipping out of bed in the middle of the night leaving Françoise, his wife, sleeping peacefully while he went downstairs and out into the garden where Claire would be waiting for him: under her dress, or coat she would be naked, then they would fuck there on the grass under the starry sky, their passion exacerbated by the thought that Françoise might wake up and discover them.

Inevitably, sooner or later, they would progress to doing it in Michel's house, or Claire's bungalow, increasing the risk to enhance their pleasure.

219

Where would it all end? He wondered as, his penis having returned to its normal state, he resumed his walk. In discovery, sooner or later, without a doubt. And then what? Divorce?

Two marriages would come to an end, but hadn't they both really ended years ago? Françoise had long since ceased to be interested in anything except her career. As for Maurice, Michel knew from personal contact with the man that he never thought about anything but making money. Two people less interested in sex it would be difficult to imagine! Michel didn't condemn them: they were, he reflected, victims of a society which had become pathologically obsessed with the notion that acquiring material possessions is the only end worth pursuing.

In the early hours of the following morning, Michel awoke to find Françoise crying. She lay in bed beside him, her body shaking with grief.

He touched her warm shoulder gently and said, 'Francie! Whatever's the matter?'

Immediately she turned to face him and came into his arms. A tear-stained cheek pressed against his.

'What is it?' he asked, long suppressed feelings of tenderness rushing to the surface.

'I can't bear it!' Françoise sobbed.

'But what's the matter?' Michel repeated.

'All this coldness which has come between us,' she wailed. 'You don't seem to be interested in anything but your books and your writing . . . You don't love me any more!' She lay beside him in the darkness, sniffing lugubriously.

Michel's heart was wrung by his wife's grief. He had never before known her to be so sensitive, so vulnerable.

He pulled the poor woman even closer to him, kissing her tear-wet cheeks, stroking her back through the flimsy nightdress, whispering reassuring words.

Most men find that women's tears are one of the most potent of aphrodisiacs, and Michel proved to be no exception.

Françoise was still a very attractive woman and as he held her body close to his, Michel could smell her warm womanly odour and feel her gently swelling breasts pressing against his chest. His prick stiffened.

Françoise was aware of what was happening, for she could feel the now rigid organ pressing against her belly. Her arms tightened around Michel's neck; she kissed him passionately.

Of course, the next thing that happened was that Michel put his hand up under the nightie and started to finger his wife's pussy. Françoise moaned with pleasure; Michel felt her fingers stroking his quivering penis.

Then, of course, it wasn't long before Michel climbed between Françoise's thighs, which opened wide to welcome him, and introduced his stiff member into her wet, burning love-sheath.

They fucked for a long time, there in the big double bed! At one stage they threw off the bedclothes because their exertions were making them sweat profusely. They fucked both passionately and tenderly, striving hard to give each other pleasure.

At length, Françoise came, gasping and moaning, followed almost immediately by Michel, who shot his seed into his wife's warm depths in quick spurts.

For a long time afterwards Michel lay on his back in the darkness, while Françoise lay snuggled up against him, her steady breathing indicating how deeply, how satisfyingly asleep she was.

He felt confused by what had happened, and not a little guilty. We really know nothing about people, he reflected, and the closer they are to us the less we understand them! The more familiar the situation, the less we realize what is going on. The sudden revelation of Françoise's vulnerability had really quite shaken him.

Then there was the question of how the present turn of events would affect his relationship with Claire. Could he still go on meeting her? Could he bear not seeing her? But if Françoise found out it would hurt her terribly, that had become quite clear tonight. But he had much more in common with Claire that he did with Françoise; however, Françoise *was* his wife! And even if he did not love her passionately, he still felt a great deal of tenderness for her, that had become quite clear tonight too!

So the tormenting thoughts continued to whirl round inside the poor man's aching head.

Michel still hadn't found a solution to the problem when he got up at six o'clock to go downstairs and put the coffee on. He wondered, however, whether one night Françoise might like to make love outside on the grass, just like in *Madame Bovary* . . .